THE SLOW RISE OF CLARA DANIELS

CHRISTY ENGLISH

For Maggie and Connie, two extraordinary women.

PROLOGUE

LOS ANGELES, 2019

THE NOISE OF THE CROWD BEYOND THE DOORS OF CLARA'S CAR WAS like the dull roar of the ocean at a distance. The sound rose and fell in waves, cresting as each luxury car approached the front of the theatre, and the celebrity it carried stepped into the light.

Clara leaned back against the leather seat of her limousine. She watched through the tinted windows as the paparazzi jostled for position beyond the red cord, fighting each other like sharks that scented blood. They had gathered to see the rich and famous come to her movie's premiere, to pick away at the flesh that fed them. Clara sighed. She had learned long ago that the press was a leech on the body of Hollywood that could not be pulled off.

Nick, her young co-star, leaned across her to get a better glimpse of the photographers beyond the windows, pressing against her and wrinkling her gown. This was his first premiere, and along the edges of his mind, Clara could feel his excitement mingled with the sharp bite of fear as he looked out at the sea of faces beyond the glass.

Clara felt a touch of almost maternal pride at how beautiful he was. She brushed Nick's blond bangs out of his eyes. With the film released, in a month's time, if not sooner, their liaison would be over. She would always think of him fondly. In spite of the age listed in his press release, he was barely eighteen.

She found herself wishing Nick wasn't vapid, that some spark of intelligence might light his eyes so she could speak with him, if not with true intimacy, at least as an equal.

That impossibility made her laugh at herself, and Nick turned to smile at her. She strengthened her mental shields under the heat of his gaze. She knew better than to read his thoughts. She always made a point of tuning them out. The empty canyon of his mind was too depressing to contemplate.

Clara heard the thoughts of the people in the crowd. Their minds were a low roar, a jumble of noise that made almost no sense. The thoughts of the people outside her car flowed past like an incoming tide. She relaxed into it and allowed herself to be buoyed by it. She let her mind float on the surface of that great ocean, the ocean she'd swum in all her life.

Nick adjusted the tie of his tuxedo, and she kissed him.

"Don't worry," she said. "You'll be fine."

Someone opened her car door and there was no more time to talk. Clara stepped out into the glare of the lights, blinded by flash bulbs. She held her ground until her eyes adjusted to the onslaught. Then she moved forward, smiling.

Nick followed her out of the car. He flashed his shy smile for the photographers, pushing his bangs out of his eyes with his trademark boyish gesture, but Clara knew where her bread was buttered. She stared past the press, to the bleachers, where her public sat waiting for her. If she had her way, the fans would be up front, and the press could take their chances.

She turned to the bleachers and gave them a dazzling smile. People began to scream her name, waving and shrieking. Clara waved back at them with one long sweep of her arm. She turned so that her public could get a good glimpse of her sequined gown. Her back was bare, and the gown swept down into a scoop of soft material just above the curve of her hips. She could hear the women murmuring to each other in approval. The men also approved, but they were silent.

With homage paid to her public, the people who kept food on her table and her pool heated, Clara turned to the press.

"Clara! Over here!"

"What's your next picture?"

"Who's that guy, Clara?"

"Are you two engaged?"

Clara took Nick's arm. The boy was starting to get overwhelmed. Even with his ego, a full press corps was tough to take the first time. And the paparazzi weren't speaking to him.

She smiled at the press, giving them a good view of the back of her gown, before drawing Nick toward the door of the theater. A bank of television cameras greeted them there, and Clara stopped to give a few one sentence interviews. She knew her job, and she was good at it. The television media were worth cultivating.

"Clara." A woman from *Entertainment Now* extended a microphone. "We understand that you and Nick have been very close since making *Shout!* together."

Clara smiled her mysterious smile, showing very few teeth. Nick stared manfully into the cameras. She could feel his terror through the stiffness in his arm.

"Nick and I had a great time working together. I hope we get to do it again." Clara's voice caressed the words of the last sentence as she ran her hand over Nick's arm.

Her touch soothed him, and she felt him relax.

She drew him forward and spoke to a few more reporters before they made it into the theater.

Once they were inside, Nick exhaled. "Holy shit. That was wild."

Clara smiled, brushing the perpetual lock of hair off his forehead.

She kissed him. "You did well."

He smiled down at her like a child who'd just been handed a sweet. "So, we'll be on TV tonight, huh?"

Clara's smile slipped a notch. "I'd say that's a safe bet."

1

PALM SPRINGS, 2009

THE LAST TIME CLARA SAW HER AUNT APRIL WAS ON HER TWELFTH birthday. She was skipping stones in the desert, when she heard the wheels of the rented Lincoln on the sunbaked gravel of the circular driveway. The sun had been up for hours, and soon it would be too hot to play in the desert any longer. Clara ran into the front yard of her mother's estate and hid herself behind a pinon tree. Her aunt stepped out of the car, offering the keys to the man whose job it was to park all visiting vehicles in the estate's ten-car garage.

Clara stood, breathing in the crisp scent of the tree until the man drove away. She emerged then, silently taking in the sight of her aunt. April was even more beautiful than Clara remembered, the milky skin of her face framing her green eyes. April laughed.

"Where did you come from, Clara? You're as quiet as a native."

"Which tribe?" Clara asked.

April laughed again but didn't answer. She put her arms around Clara. The girl stood unyielding until she remembered that to be hugged, one had to hug back. She relaxed and felt the tension run out of her body like water. She wasn't used to being touched, but she reminded herself that April was different. April loved her.

She pressed her face against April's silk suit and breathed in the

5

scent of her aunt's light perfume. The silk against her cheek was the color of the peeled avocados her mother loved.

She knew April had come for her birthday and had wanted to surprise her. Clara gave April one of her rare smiles. Her aunt blinked in the light of that smile, smoothing the girl's hair away from her face.

"Let's get out of this heat."

Aunt April squeezed Clara's shoulder, and the girl moved ahead of her into her mother's mansion. The foyer was cool, and the marble floors were polished under their feet. Clara could hear the faint hum of an air conditioner somewhere in the house.

"Where's your mother, Clara?"

The girl shrugged one shoulder, feigning indifference. "I don't know."

"Is she here?"

Clara met her aunt's eyes. "No."

April smoothed a strand of hair out of her eye. "Well, we'll have lunch together, then."

Clara relished her aunt's touch as April took her hand.

They sat in the conservatory facing the terraced gardens. The plush furniture had bright white cushions, and the harsh sunlight was filtered by the glass, though the heat wasn't kept out. It was always hot in the conservatory, but it was Clara's favorite room in the house. Past the gardens, beyond the lawns and pinon trees, she could see the desert shimmering.

The housekeeper, Carol, brought in sandwiches and lemonade, and Clara asked for slices of the apple cake that the cook had baked for her that morning, along with the herbal tea April loved.

Clara watched her aunt from the corner of her eye. She saw April's jaw tighten as she looked out over the desert, and she knew that her aunt was angry. She couldn't read April's thoughts, though, just as she couldn't read her mother's. Beyond the one question that Clara longed to have an answer for, she was sure her mother had no interesting thoughts in her head. However, she wished she could see behind her aunt's eyes, if only for a moment.

6

Clara met April's eyes, and blinked. She had been caught staring.

But Aunt April only smiled. "I've brought you something."

Clara attempted a feeble joke. "A filter I can wear over my head, to keep out people's thoughts?"

April looked over her shoulder, but no servant was nearby to hear what Clara had said. She knew her aunt had a superstitious fear of referring to the family gift.

"If they ever make one, I'll order you the first off the assembly line."

"They'll never make one. No one knows what we can do."

April shifted in her plush chair, crossing her legs, and met Clara's gaze. "No. They don't know."

Clara knew she must never speak of her gift in front of anyone, and she never did. Only with her aunt. April was the only person in the world she could trust to always be there and never to betray her.

She looked gleeful, like the child she was. "What did you bring me?"

April smiled, brushing a strand of ash blonde hair back from her eyes. Her long hair was caught up in an elegant twist, but wisps had come loose, framing her face.

"Maybe we should eat our lunch first."

Clara laughed at her aunt's teasing. "What did you bring me?"

Clara moved to sit next to her aunt on the sofa, and April stroked the crown of Clara's head. April reached into the shopping bag leaning against her chair and drew out a box wrapped in fine white paper. A huge pink ribbon covered the front of the package, and Clara glowered. She hated the color pink.

April laughed when she saw her face. "I knew you'd hate the ribbon, but the store didn't have anything else."

Clara lifted the present onto her lap as carefully as if it were a holy relic. She didn't want to tear the paper, but to sit and look at her birthday present, making the moment of anticipation stretch before her. She knew she wasn't going to get another gift. But Clara also knew that no pleasure was made to last, so with a swift glance at April, she tore the paper.

The white paper and pink ribbon fell on the hardwood floor as Clara's fingers lingered over the box. She took a deep breath, savoring the moment. She opened the box slowly, drawing the tissue paper back gently so she wouldn't tear it.

Nestled in the paper was a cashmere sweater the same shade of green as her eyes. Clara took a shallow breath, bringing the sweater up to her cheek, the box falling at her feet. She breathed in the scent of the soft fabric, which smelled like her aunt's perfume.

"Aunt April… it's beautiful."

Clara was rarely awed by anything, but the sweater in her hands was the most beautiful present she had ever been given.

"You can wear it when you come back to New York, and we go to the Russian Tea Room."

Clara didn't answer but fingered the soft material.

Aunt April slid her manicured fingertips into her leather handbag. "I have something else for you, too."

Clara's eyes sparkled as she took the envelope her aunt handed her. She opened it, and an airline ticket fluttered out and landed in her lap. When she picked it up, she saw that it was a one-way ticket to New York.

She looked at her aunt, an eyebrow raised.

April spoke in a rush, her words a jumble of sound. "I want you to live with me."

The floor opened at her feet as Clara fingered the paper in her hands. It was a way out of her mother's house. An escape from the man her mother was marrying.

Clara remembered the last time she'd gone to New York. She had flown out alone that Christmas, her mother and her fiancé left far behind in Palm Springs. Aunt April had met her at the airport, and for the entire week of her visit, they had done only things that made her happy.

She looked down at the ticket in her hand. April wanted to give her a new life, a life like the week she'd had in New York.

Clara thought of Darren then, the man her mother intended to marry. He was ten years younger than her mother, with a tennis player's build and blue eyes. His eyes looked as if they belonged to a man with a soul, unless you could read what went on behind them.

Tears came into her eyes, and for the first time since her father died, Clara couldn't swallow for the pain in her throat. The airline ticket blurred in her hand. She blinked hard to see past her tears.

She forced herself to speak, though her voice shook. "Does Mom know that you want to take me?"

"We'll tell her when she comes home."

Clara thought of her mother's light laugh, of her clear blue eyes that took the whole world at face value. Jessica almost never looked past a person's eyes to the thoughts in the mind behind them. Clara didn't know what would happen to her mother if she had to face wicked people alone. She imagined her mother left alone with Darren, and held herself very still, forcing herself not to breathe so she wouldn't shudder.

She did not think Darren meant her mother harm. He was walking toxic waste, but she hadn't seen any evil in intentions behind his eyes when he looked at her mother. But she would never be sure unless she stayed and watched over him.

"I can't go with you." Her hand didn't shake as she held out the ticket.

April looked at it for a long moment, before she took it back.

"Will you think about it, Clara?" Her aunt's voice was gentle and low. Clara could hear the misery in it.

Pain filled her own vision, burning away what was left of her tears.

Clara hardened her voice to keep from showing it. "I have thought about it. I can't leave Mom alone with him."

"Clara, she hasn't given you a moment's thought, and she won't take care of you once he's in this house. Do you understand that?"

April's voice was low but took on an urgency that Clara had never heard before—the urgency of desperation. She hadn't known that her aunt was capable of feeling desperate. For the first time, she understood how much April loved her.

She took April's hand, careful not to touch the diamonds on her aunt's fingers, and spoke calmly, as if to a younger child.

"Mom needs me here to take care of her."

They sat staring at each other over a plate of sandwiches and a cooling pot of tea. April reached out and brushed her fingertips over Clara's face. "If you change your mind, you can call me anytime, day or night, and I'll come for you."

Clara's stomach clenched, and the pit opened at her feet again. There was finality in her aunt's voice.

April brushed her well-manicured hands over Clara's hair, smoothing out the blonde strands. She looked at her niece as if she were memorizing her face.

"I'd better go before your mother gets back."

Clara heard her own words, and they sounded detached, like the voice of a stranger.

"All right."

April pulled Clara against her and kissed her cheek. A little of her lipstick came off on Clara's skin. She didn't relax against her aunt's body, but breathed the scent of her perfume, to remember it. She knew April had no intention of ever coming back.

"I love you, Clara. Happy birthday."

April walked away. Clara listened to the staccato beat of her aunt's high heels as they struck the marble in the foyer. She heard Carol open the door, and she stood listening for the sound of April's car as she drove away. The house was silent except for the tick of the grandfather clock standing like a sentinel in the marble hallway.

2

LOS ANGELES, 2019

CLARA STOPPED HER MASERATI AT THE STUDIO GATE, SMILING AT the slouching guard on duty. He straightened and lifted his cap to her, bowing at the waist as if she were the Queen of England.

"Go right through, Miss Daniels."

Clara let her voice find its lowest register. "Thank you, Derek."

She drove too fast around the huge barn-like studio buildings, playing a game of tag with herself. How close could she come to a producer before he would move? Some even shouted at her and waved a fist, before seeing who she was and falling silent. She left the working schlubs alone.

Her music was loud, but she could still pick up a few stray thoughts as she drove past them. Most were murderous, until they saw her face.

She stopped her car in the space painted with her name. She turned off her music reluctantly and steeled herself for the ordeal to come.

Clara stepped out of her car, and there was a lackey waiting for her. A young woman in sloppy shorts and a stained t-shirt with the name of a TV movie written on it.

"Miss Daniels, Mr. Willoughby is expecting you."

Clara didn't smile. "All right."

She reached into her bag for a cigarette, striding towards the stucco office building on her left. The woman trotted beside her, her face a mask of embarrassed misery.

"Miss Daniels, can I get you anything?"

"No."

Clara stopped long enough to light her cigarette, but before she could strike a flame from her lighter, the woman extended a match. Clara really saw her for the first time and looked behind her eyes. In spite of years with the studio, in spite of the fact that her every working day was full of humiliation and misery, this woman worshipped Clara as a goddess on the earth.

The woman didn't move, and the match burned lower. Clara knew she would allow her fingers to burn off before she would put the match out. Clara leaned down slowly, almost casually, and lit her cigarette from the fire at the woman's fingertips. She blew the flame out just before the woman's fingers got burned.

Clara smiled then, the slow smile she was famous for. The woman blinked as if dazzled by the sun. She fished into the woman's mind and found her name.

"Thanks for the light, Peg."

The woman stood silent as Clara moved past her into the studio building where Bob Willoughby waited in his office on the fourth floor.

Bob Willoughby, the head of Barnett Studios, sat at the end of a long mahogany table, smoking a cigar. He hastily put the cigar out and rose to his feet when Clara entered the room. His assistant, Phil, was at her side immediately, taking her handbag and offering her a glass of orange juice.

Clara took the glass and surrendered her bag without comment, her eyes fixed on Willoughby's face. Willoughby's new Vice President of Marketing drew out a chair for her and Clara sat, the slit in her skirt revealing her long leg, up to her thigh. The marketing VP's gaze rested on her legs for a moment, before he took his seat next to Willoughby.

Clara tried to look into the VP's mind to see whether or not his calm was a façade but found that she couldn't. His mind was closed to her. She frowned. That had never happened to her before, except with the other women of her family.

The Vice President of Marketing smiled at her as if he knew what she was thinking. Her frown deepened. He couldn't have been older than twenty-four. He had a lot of power for someone so young, to be sitting in a meeting with her and Bob. She wondered briefly if she had seen him somewhere before.

Clara let her frown fade and allowed herself. She wondered why Willoughby had brought him in, perhaps in a vain attempt to cajole her. Bob must be under the false impression that she was slipping.

She turned the strength of her gaze on Willoughby and he blinked, caught off guard. He swallowed hard and focused on the papers in front of him.

"Well, Clara, I appreciate you coming in today."

She smiled then. "I know you do, Bob."

"Yes, well—"

The studio head coughed convulsively, and his assistant silently handed him a glass of water. Willoughby drank it in three swallows and handed the empty glass back to Phil. For a moment, Clara thought he might mop his brow like one of the characters in the stupid films she made, but he didn't do anything so obvious. He forced himself to meet her eyes, and she caught a glimpse of the man who had taken a chance on hiring her four years before.

"Clara, the people on the board are concerned about your next project."

"Really?"

She kept her voice deceptively even and pleasant, sipping her juice. It was slightly sour.

"Yes. They're afraid the market is too tight for a costume drama. They want to put you in a space thriller instead."

Clara was silent for the span of a minute. She waited to see if anyone else in the room would speak again. When they didn't, she extended her hand and Phil was there immediately, placing a lit cigarette between her fingers. She took a slow draw of tobacco, her gaze fixed firmly on Willoughby.

"And what do you think, Bob?"

Willoughby looked surprised at the even tone of her voice, he and took a deep breath. She could feel his fear from where she sat. She wasn't used to seeing Bob Willoughby afraid. She felt her temper rising.

"You know I'm not paid to think, Clara. Not creatively, anyway. These men know the markets. They feel that a costume drama will flop and lose more studio money than we can afford."

Willoughby shifted in his chair. He looked down at his papers and shuffled them. Clara got a flash into his mind. They were blank pages.

She kept her voice low, ignoring the marketing VP, who cleared his throat, almost as if he intended to speak. She stared hard at Willoughby until he met her eyes.

"Are they shelving my project, Bob?"

He nodded. Clara stayed silent for a long moment, the glass of sour orange juice in her hand. The marketing VP turned to her. She saw Bob reach for his arm to silence him, but the VP ignored him, focusing his indigo blue eyes on her. For some inexplicable reason, try as she might, Clara still couldn't read what he was thinking.

"Miss Daniels, the marketing department wants you to know that we consider the shelving of this project only temporary. We've had quite a few setbacks in foreign markets, and we need to shore-up our position. We feel that if you consider the space thriller, *Blast Away*, we'll be in a better position to return to—"

Clara stood in the middle of his speech, and in one smooth motion, threw her orange juice against the wall behind his head. The crystal shattered against the wood paneling and the sour juice ran down the wall in rivulets.

She didn't look at the VP again but turned to Bob. Phil was at her side with her bag. She delicately took a last draw off her cigarette and stubbed it out in the crystal ashtray on the table. Bob's eyes were wide, and she could feel him holding his breath.

"I think you know my position on this, Bob. I'll wait for your call."

Clara turned, and Phil opened the door for her smoothly. She was out of the building and back in her car before she remembered that when she'd thrown her glass the VP hadn't even flinched.

~

"Who the hell is he?" Clara spoke into her cell, standing on her balcony overlooking Malibu Bay.

Donna spoke calmly. "I don't know, Clara, but I'll find out."

"I want his job."

"Let me find out who he is first. There may be a way around him."

Clara drew the smoke from her Turkish cigarette into her lungs.

"All right. I'll wait."

"I'll handle it, Clara. I'll call you tonight."

Clara smiled at the confidence in her manager's voice. Donna was one of the few people she respected.

"Tonight, then."

Clara laid her phone down and stared out over the Pacific. The water was a dull gray, reflecting the gray of the smog trapped over the bay. Her cigarette was lightly laced with hashish, and Clara could feel tendrils of warmth relaxing her muscles despite her fury. Her mind started to unclench as she drew in another breath of the sweet-smelling smoke. Donna would handle the little prick, whoever he was.

She slid into the Jacuzzi on her deck as Margherita brought her a glass of fruit juice.

"Thank you, Maggie."

Her little maid smiled, flashing the gold tooth that Clara had paid for. "You are welcome, miss. Would you like some lunch?"

Clara leaned back against the pool's padded edge and sighed. "No, thanks."

The older woman walked away on silent feet. Clara saw Margherita's son, Paolo, emerge from the bushes along the side of the house with clippers in his hands. His chest was slick with sweat. Paolo looked like some Toltec god emerging from the underbrush.

She smiled and spoke to him in Spanish. "Your flowers are beautiful, Paolo."

The young man said nothing but laid his gardening shears down carefully on a cedar bench. He moved with the grace of a panther as he knelt beside the pool and took her hair in his hand. Clara offered him a draw from her cigarette. He took it and cast it over the balcony rail.

"I wasn't finished with that."

Paolo said nothing. He drew her up onto the deck to lie beside him. His hands were hard on her body as he peeled away her bathing suit and started to make love to her on the sun- drenched deck. She marveled at the wonders of her life, that this beautiful man could make love to her on hard cedar planks that were so well-lacquered, she never got a splinter in her back.

3

PALM SPRINGS, 2009

Twelve-year-old Clara pulled on the too-tight collar of her pink chiffon dress. She stood next to the antique vanity table, watching as her mother put on her makeup, layer by careful layer.

Jessica Daniels was dressed in a white satin gown that clung to her figure like a second skin, skimming over her hips to swirl around her ankles. It had belonged to Clara's great-grandmother in the 1930's. She imagined that the satin would feel smooth and cool under her hand, if she had the courage to reach out and touch it. Her mother's hair was gathered in a golden chignon.

She watched as her mother smoothed gloss over her lipstick. Jessica met her daughter's gaze in the antique mirror.

"Want some lipstick, honey?"

Clara blinked. Her mother never spoke until her beauty ritual was complete. Today was an exception. Today was her mother's wedding day.

"Yes, Mom. I would."

Jessica slid over on the mahogany bench of the dressing table and laid her hand on the seat beside her.

"Sit down, honey, and I'll paint you face."

Clara sat very still, praying that no one would come in and

17

distract her mother before she finished. Jessica was so easily distracted. Many times, she had begun to make-up Clara's face, only to be interrupted by a phone call or a visit. She would rush off to speak to the adult, leaving Clara forgotten.

Today, no one came in. The phone didn't ring. Clara heard Carol, the housekeeper, call to someone in the garden below, ordering someone hired for the day to move a flower arrangement to a more convenient location. Then the old landline rang down the hall. Clara flinched, but Jessica took no notice of it. She simply brushed powder over her little girl's cheeks with unbroken concentration, as if she were creating a work of art.

Clara watched as her face was transformed in the mirror before her. Her mother used the paint sparingly, but to good effect. She didn't look made-up, but her features were clearer, more distinct. She stared at her reflection and saw for the first time that she was as beautiful as her mother was.

"You look pretty, Clara."

"Thank you, Mom."

Jessica sat for a moment, saying nothing. They stared at each other in the mirror, in silence. It was the longest that Clara had ever held her mother's gaze.

She thought Jessica might speak, that her mother might say something important before she walked down the stairs, to the man who waited for her, changing their lives forever. For a moment, Clara hoped wildly that her mother would call the whole thing off. She hoped they might run off to Cancun together, leaving Darren in the dust.

But the moment faded.

Jessica smiled brightly and stood. "Hand me my bouquet, would you, honey? We can't keep the guests waiting."

Clara stood and handed her mother the spray of white roses and calla lilies. Her voice stuck in her throat as Jessica moved to the door in her satin gown. She watched as her mother's manicured fingers turned the glass doorknob, and the door opened.

Clara could hear the noise from downstairs clearly then. Carol was bellowing to someone about moving a case of champagne out into the yard. She watched her mother give her appearance one last check in the full-length mirror before she turned and walked away.

Clara looked at herself in the full-length mirror as her mother had done. Her new makeup made her look like a painted doll. She washed it off before going downstairs. She was late, and Carol had to come and fetch her down. The ceremony was about to start.

Everywhere Clara went at her mother's wedding reception, there were people. She wanted to go walking in the desert to get away from them, but she knew that she would ruin her dress. The pink chiffon rasped against her skin, and she winced. She hated pink. Why her mother had chosen it for her, she didn't understand.

She stood under one of the tents, shaded from the hot afternoon sun. The shadows were beginning to slant across the manicured lawn behind her mother's house, over the beautiful blooming gardens. Her mother had ordered flowers flown in from all over the world to fill the terrace and to add their perfume to the tables that stretched under the white awnings. The tables overflowed with caviar from Russia, oysters from Baja, crab and lobster from Maine. Clara hated seafood, but she stood next to the table with the fish. It had been emptied for the most part, and as a result, there were fewer people surrounding it.

Clara looked longingly past the terraced gardens to the desert that stretched beyond them. Tomorrow she would pack a lunch and go into the desert for the whole day. Her mother wouldn't be there to worry. She and Darren would be in Cancun by then.

She looked up to find Darren watching her with a steady gaze from across the lawn. Clara swallowed but didn't drop his gaze. He murmured something in her mother's ear, his eyes never leaving Clara's face. Jessica smiled up at him, her lips sliding over his cheek. He took his eyes from Clara long enough to lean over and kiss her mother's mouth—the kind of kiss that, in Clara's opinion, should have stayed in their bedroom.

She watched as Darren crossed the wide expanse of lawn. She

didn't turn away or try to avoid him. Avoiding the unpleasant only postponed the inevitable. Clara preferred to face her battles head-on. She didn't blink or smile as he stopped in front of her.

"Hi, Clara. You having fun?"

She shrugged one shoulder and looked down at the few remaining crab legs displayed on a bank of ice. Darren reached over and took one. He cracked the shell with his teeth before drawing the flesh out with his tongue. He winked at her, casting the remains onto a passing servant's tray, then smiled at her, his white teeth gleaming in his tanned face.

Clara watched him with a sort of sick fascination. She didn't yet understand how a person's face could be so different from the thoughts going on behind his eyes.

Darren was attractive, with a glowing healthiness that led people to believe he was wholesome. Because of the family gift, Clara knew he was far from it. She wondered how her mother couldn't know. Clara's eyes widened slightly as she considered, for the first time, the possibility that her mother knew exactly what Darren was and wanted him anyway.

Darren looked down at her for a long moment, letting the silence stretch between them. Clara held her breath, hoping he might say something stupid and move on. He didn't. He simply kept staring at her.

He reached out and smoothed her hair back from her cheek. She had left it down for the wedding, and the pink flower she wore over one ear matched the color of her dress. The pads of his fingers slid over her smooth skin, and his hand ran down her cheek to cup her chin.

To someone watching, it would look like an innocent caress offered to a child. Clara knew better. She felt the warmth of his palm and heard the thoughts behind his clear blue eyes. She met his gaze and didn't pull away.

"Will you be bored here all by yourself next week, kiddo?" His voice was casual and light.

He took his hand away, reaching for a glass of champagne. He tipped the glass back, and she watched the liquid slide down his throat. He drank the champagne in three swallows, his eyes never leaving her face.

She kept her voice deceptively calm. "No."

"Good." His tone had a hearty quality to it that many men used when speaking with children.

She knew he didn't see her as a child.

Jessica beckoned to him from the steps of the terrace. She blew Clara a kiss and waved to her from her marble perch.

"I guess we'd better go meet your mom."

Darren's gaze shifted from her to Jessica. The hand he had laid on her arm fell away.

He was afraid to really touch her. He would never try to get her alone. He wouldn't risk losing Jessica's money. At least Clara's mother had had the sense to make him sign a prenuptial agreement. An airtight one, the lawyer had assured her, as Clara listened from the hallway.

Clara smiled up at him and took his arm. Darren's eyes shifted to her face, and he must have seen something of her thoughts there. For the first time since she'd known him, she felt fear run through him. He knew she saw him for what he was.

Clara walked with her mother's husband, clinging to his arm as she'd seen other women do to their male escorts. She broke away from him when they met her mother on the steps and leaned up to meet her mother's kiss.

Jessica's lips were soft against her cheek. She ran her hand over her daughter's hair, and Clara stared into her beautiful blue eyes. Not for the first time, she wished fervently that she could read her mother's mind as she could everyone else's. As it was, she felt as if she were the adult and Jessica, the child.

"Take care of yourself, Clara."

"I always do, Mom."

Darren drew Jessica away then, and the guests surged around them as they went into the house, blocking her mother from her sight. Clara knew they would converge on the front porch to throw birdseed at the couple as they left. She could hear the laughter of the crowd from where she stood. She could feel that only some of their merriment and good wishes were false.

Clara didn't follow them. She sat on the marble steps, heedless of her scratchy skirt, and watched as the caterers began to clear away the reception food. The edges of the nearest tent flapped in the breeze, and she leaned into the wind that brought with it the scent of the desert. The sun was setting low over the sand beyond her mother's lawn. Clara watched the light fade, swiping away the lone tear that slid down her cheek.

4

MALIBU, 2019

Clara leaned back on the divan in her living room. She sipped her cognac, watching the sun set over Malibu Bay. The pollution refracted the rays of the sun, so the colors were subdued in their brilliance as the red disk sank into the ocean.

Her house was completely quiet except for the sound of the sea. Paolo and his mother had gone to their homes across town. Clara wouldn't have people in the house at night. She liked to sleep without being awakened by other people's dreams.

She listened idly to the silence, letting it pool around her and cocoon her. She still hadn't heard from her manager regarding the asshat she'd met earlier that day, but she wasn't worried. Donna knew her job. The marketing VP would be pounding the streets by morning.

Clara turned away from the sunset when she heard the soft chimes of her doorbell.

No one ever rang her doorbell. Whenever someone came to see her, the guard called up from her neighborhood's front gate. No one ever got in.

She drew her filmy blouse around her as she rose. She wore an emerald green silk dress under it, with thin spaghetti straps clinging to her shoulders. Clara loved to hear the sound of silk whisper as she moved in the silence. All shades of silence were precious to her, because they were so rare.

She moved slowly to the front door. Maybe Margherita had forgotten something.

Clara fumbled with the locks and swung open the heavy mahogany door. The marketing VP stood on her porch. He was dressed in light chinos and a navy blue blazer. The suit from the office was gone. His eyes were hidden behind sunglasses. She couldn't hear his thoughts. He stood with her, a partner in the blessed silence.

"Hello." His voice was deep, and the sound of it soothed her as the sound of the sea did.

He took off his glasses and quirked an eyebrow at her before letting his gaze slide down her body. His eyes lingered on her breasts before returning to her face. Clara laughed in spite of herself.

"If you've come to beg for your job, you've started off badly."

He smiled. "I never beg."

His eyes were a deep cerulean blue. Clara wondered idly if he wore contact lenses to give them that particular hue, and then realized that he didn't. That blue was real. He watched her in silence.

"How did you get past the gate?"

"I drove through it."

Clara spoke quietly, keeping her voice low. "Well, you can drive back through it."

She started to close the door, but he stepped forward and stopped her. To her surprise, she let him.

"I'll drive back through it after I come in for a drink, and we talk."

"We have nothing to say."

"I do."

He pushed past her, gently. She couldn't believe his audacity. He stepped into her foyer and looked up at the skylight above his head. The stars were coming out in the dark blue sky, and when Clara looked up, too, she saw that the night sky was the exact shade of his eyes.

Clara closed the door again and locked it. She leaned back against it, watching to see what he would do next.

He stood still in the middle of her foyer and looked at her. "Maybe we should turn on a light."

She knew she should be angry. There was a security button hidden in the paneling of the door. All she had to do was touch it to bring the police and have this man thrown in jail. She didn't touch it, though. Instead, she kept looking at him.

Clara was surprised at herself. She wasn't even annoyed. The VP watched her quietly, saying nothing, as if waiting for her to pass judgment. For some reason, Clara felt oddly safe with him, at ease in a way she never was with other people. There was an elusive quality to his confidence that reminded her of herself.

Clara tried again to look into his mind. It wasn't blank. It was a heavy door, locked against her.

He smiled, and suddenly she remembered the last time she'd felt this at ease with another human being. It had been with her Aunt April, at noon on her twelfth birthday, the last time she'd ever seen her.

Clara reminded herself how that meeting had ended, but for some reason she wasn't troubled as she looked into his face. He seemed to be a kindred spirit. The idea that there was someone like her anywhere was an illusion, but it was a nice illusion. Clara decided to indulge herself in it, if only for one night.

She forced herself to take her eyes off him and to walk past him into her living room. Her house was one story, one of its arms reaching back into her bedroom, the other into the huge kitchen, which she used only for parties. She knew Margherita had left something in the oven, though she had no idea what.

"Are you hungry?" she asked him.

"I am."

Clara led him back into the kitchen and turned on a light as they entered. She could feel his eyes on her as if his gaze were hands. She opened the oven and found a pot roast with new potatoes and baby carrots nestled next to it.

Clara smiled and pulled it out of the oven. "I think my maid knew I was going to have company."

He said nothing but kept watching her as she moved around her kitchen. She found two plates after a little digging, and two wine glasses. She pulled a bottle of Bordeaux down from her wine rack and turned to find him standing beside her.

He took it from her. "Let me."

"All right."

She dug around for a while longer and found a corkscrew, which she handed to him. He opened the wine and poured it while she watched. His hands were deft and never shook. She wondered if he had any idea who she was.

"Do you know who I am?"

He moved slowly across the kitchen and handed her a glass. "I do. But you don't know me."

Clara took a sip, her eyes never leaving his. "Yes, I do. You're the little prick I had fired today."

He laughed out loud, and she found herself smiling as she listened to him. He seemed genuinely amused. He sounded happy. Clara had never known anyone who was happy. She couldn't read his thoughts to know if he was lying. He was a complete blank to her, except for his eyes.

He took a knife and started slicing the roast. He put food on both the plates she'd found, precisely, as if he had served food all his life.

He picked up his plate and glass. "Where should we eat?"

"Here, I guess." Clara gestured to the huge island in the center of the kitchen.

Its wooden top gleamed with polish. Two stools stood against it, and he sat down on one and started eating casually, as if he were in his mother's kitchen. Clara looked around the room she almost never entered and started laughing.

"I can't believe I'm in here with you."

He looked up at her. "Aren't you hungry?"

"Yes."

"Then eat."

No one had given her an order in years, but this man did it casually as he lifted his wine glass to his lips and drank. She watched him swallow and then lick his lips before he took another bite. She stood staring at him until he met her gaze.

His voice was gentle. "Sit down and eat, Clara."

She pulled up the second stool and raised her fork to her mouth. The carrots were succulent with butter and some sort of pepper. She tasted the roast beef next, and it seemed to melt on her tongue. It was the best food she'd ever eaten, and she had eaten in the best restaurants in the world. Margherita was a wonderful cook, but Clara knew that wasn't it. It was the company. She felt as if she had stepped out of her normal life and was in a separate space, someplace she'd never been before, a place of peace.

She looked over at him. "What's your name?"

He raised his glass again and took another sip of wine. "I wondered when it would occur to you to ask that question."

"Well?"

His blue eyes sparkled with laughter as he smiled at her. "My name is Fred."

Clara almost choked on a bite of potato. "Fred?"

"That's right."

"Your name's not Bruce or Steve or Lance or something like that?"

He poured more wine into both of their glasses. "No. It's Fred."

Clara started to laugh. She felt a deep belly laugh rise through her chest, and it came out of her mouth before she could stop it. She gripped the edge of the bar, convulsively, her knuckles turning white. She couldn't hear herself think. All she could do was laugh.

"Why is my name so funny?"

She took a deep breath, trying to stop. She wiped the tears from her eyes. She hadn't laughed so freely since she was a child, playing in the desert of Palm Springs, chasing her shadow across empty sands.

She looked at the man sitting in her kitchen. He had finished his dinner and was watching her with no hint of fear or awkwardness. Clara sat staring back at him for a long time, until it occurred to her to speak.

"I don't know why it's funny. I don't know why you're here. No one gets into my house uninvited."

"Yet here I am."

"Here you are."

His gaze didn't waver from her face as he smiled at her. "You don't remember me, do you?"

Clara took a deep breath. She thought for a moment that she might start laughing again, but the danger had passed.

"Of course, I do. We met in Bob's office on your last day with Barnett Studios."

Fred let her jibe go without lifting an eyebrow. "No. We met before today."

"No, we didn't."

Fred's stare didn't leave her face. "You were seventeen. You were wearing a green dress that matched the color of your eyes. You were hunting men at Stan Hendrickson's party. You bagged me."

Clara frowned, casting her mind back. She had been to so many parties when she'd first started her career, then had quickly discovered that Hollywood parties were always the same dramas played out by the same characters. She found that she got more done working with an up-and-coming executive named Bob Willoughby, so she had stopped going to parties.

She didn't remember ever seeing Fred at any of them.

"Did you get a face lift or something?"

It was Fred's turn to laugh. He almost choked on his Bordeaux and he spluttered, setting his wine glass down.

When he could speak, he wiped his eyes. "No, I've never had surgery. I was working for Stan as an intern at the time. I got paid nothing, but I got to sneak into his parties."

"How old were you then?"

"About twenty-two."

Clara shook her head, dismissing the idea. "There's no way I would have slept with someone so young. You had no pull."

"I don't think pull was what you were looking for that night."

She narrowed her eyes, wishing she could see into his mind. She thought back on her early meanderings. There were a few nights when she had indulged herself in hunting men sexually simply for the pleasure of it. Maybe she had slept with him.

"Did we go to your place or mine?" she asked.

"Neither. We went into the guest bathroom on the third floor."

Clara laughed, beginning to relax. "Yeah, that sounds like me."

His face darkened, his blue eyes deepening to indigo.

"So, you had a lot of lovers, I take it?"

"I still do."

Clara watched him, surprised to see a muscle leap in his jaw. If she hadn't known he was trying to manipulate her, she would have thought he was genuinely jealous.

She watched him swallow and take a deep breath. He seemed to get a grip on himself in that moment, because his jaw unclenched and his eyes warmed.

"Maybe that will change."

"I doubt it."

Fred's eyes didn't waver from her face. Clara felt as if they were deep pools of indigo that she could dive into and hide from the world. She frowned at the seductive thought. She wasn't a woman who hid from anything.

"Why did you shelve my project?"

He straightened on his stool before he bent to pour her more wine. Clara stopped him by covering her wine glass with her hand. When she was with a stranger, two glasses were her limit.

"Answer me."

Fred put the wine bottle down and looked into her eyes. Clara kept her mind focused on her question so she would not get distracted again by the luxury of having a normal conversation without hearing the other person's thoughts, and so she wouldn't lose her focus in the blue of his eyes.

"Your project was in my way."

"How so?"

Fred stood. "Do you really want to talk about this here?"

Clara stood to face him. "Yes."

He sighed softly and pushed his hand through his thick black hair. "I'm moving into a new position of power at the studio. In order for that to happen, your film had to make way for another project. I'm sorry about that."

Fred met her gaze with simple honesty. Clara couldn't remember the last time a man had been honest with her, besides Bob Willoughby. With Bob, she could see his honesty written in his thoughts. This man was still a blank. She had built her life trusting only what people thought, not what they said.

"I can't tell what you're thinking."

"I know. You like it, don't you?"

Clara smiled at his audacity. "Yes."

He took her arm and steered her back into the main part of the house. The light from the kitchen spilled onto the plush carpet of the dark living room. Yachts on Malibu Bay could be seen bobbing outside the plate glass windows. His hand lingered on her arm, then slid to her waist.

"I could have you fired," she said.

"No, you couldn't."

His hand was warm on her back. She could feel it through the thin silk of her dress.

"But you could make things difficult for me," he said. "I'm asking you not to."

"Not get you fired?"

She felt rather than saw him smile in the semi-dark.

"No. I'm asking you not to complicate my deal. Let me shelve your project. I'll make it up to you later."

"Oh, really? How?"

He slid his hand up her back, his fingers caressing her shoulder blades through the gauze of her blouse.

"I'll be in a position to do you a favor in the future, if you ever need one."

"I don't need favors."

Clara felt her breath come short, and she had to force herself to concentrate on his words instead of his hands.

"Well, do it as a favor to me, then."

She laughed low in her throat. "If you know who I am, you know that I never give out favors."

"Not for frcc."

Fred's lips were soft at her temple. He kissed her, brushing her lips with a feather-light touch, waiting to see if she would object. He was giving her the opportunity to say no.

Clara didn't say no. She turned to him, brushing her lips against the edge of his jaw. He stood still for a long moment, letting her hands slide inside his jacket, up his back, to his shoulders. She brushed his lips lightly with hers, and then pulled away, waiting to see what he would do.

"I've never made love with a screen goddess before."

She laughed low in her throat. "You can't possibly expect me to believe that."

His hands glided down her back, playing against her muscles. One palm moved up her arm to toy with the spaghetti strap of her dress.

"I didn't say I haven't had an actress or two. Just never a goddess."

Clara laughed again, a deep belly laugh that shook her whole body.

She leaned against him for support. "Don't tell me you write screenplays, too."

She felt him smile against her hair as his lips brushed the top of her head.

"Not yet."

He moved his hands over her shoulders, and her blouse dropped onto the floor at her feet. Her laughter died in her throat as he leaned down and covered her mouth with his. The touch of his lips was light at first, until she opened her lips under his. The taste of him made her sway on her feet, and she clutched his jacket. He drew her close and kept kissing her, running his hands over her shoulders until the straps of her dress slid away under his palms.

"I want you." Clara's voice was hoarse in her own ears.

She couldn't remember making such an admission to any of her lovers. She must be losing her mind.

Fred pulled her down onto the soft carpet that covered her living room floor, and for the next few minutes Clara forgot about her career, her movie, even that she couldn't see into this man's mind. She simply let herself enjoy the moment.

When the sexual storm was over, she let her cheek rest on his chest, listening to the thunder of his heartbeat. They lay together in silence for a long time before Clara spoke.

"I remember you now."

"I don't doubt it."

She laughed at him. "And that isn't my payment, so don't think it is."

He bit her gently on the neck until she shrieked like a teenager.

"No?"

"No."

"What do you want instead?"

Clara smiled, running her hands idly across the hard muscles of his chest, feeling expansive.

"I'll let you know."

Fred came out of the shower as Clara picked up the phone.

"Hi, Donna."

"Hi, yourself. You sound better."

"Better than yesterday."

"About that VP, Clara—"

"I want you to forget him, Donna. I've decided to let him go."

Fred quirked an eyebrow at her, rubbing a towel over his wet hair.

"I'm glad to hear you say that, Clara. His position at the studio is stronger than I thought. I've been gathering data on him—"

"Keep doing that, Donna. Now I want you to approach Sony with the project and see if they'll bite."

Donna shifted gears smoothly. "All right. Do you want anyone in particular to direct?"

"No. Leave the choice of director up to them as a gesture of good faith. I'll take whoever they give me, in exchange for picking up the project."

"OK. Now, if they're leery—"

"They won't be. If Stan gives you any trouble, call me."

Donna laughed. "You're right. Who am I kidding? I'll call you with the preliminaries as soon as I have them."

"Thanks, Donna." Clara laid the phone down.

"So, you're taking the project away from us?"

"Of course, I am. If you don't want the project, Sony will."

Fred smiled against her skin as he pressed a kiss to her throat. "Are you sure you won't reconsider? I only need to shelve you for a year to six months."

Clara laughed, running her hand through his still-damp hair. "Are you trying to get around me, Fred? It can't be done."

"I think we both know that isn't true."

Clara drew away from him. "Don't push it."

He took her hair in his hands and brought her toward him. "I love you, Clara."

His eyes were serious. She could see no hint of humor in them. His hands were gentle, his fingertips brushing her cheek. She knew he wasn't a psychopath, so his words were just a clumsy, ill-thought-out attempt to manipulate her. For some reason, that fact didn't make her angry. It disappointed her. At last, she knew where she stood. Even without reading his mind, she knew very well how to deal with other people's feeble attempts at manipulation, and her own disappointment.

She was almost glad he had betrayed her as she'd known he would. It had simply taken him longer than most.

She tried to keep emotion out of her voice, but she failed. Despite her best efforts and her years of strict self-governance, she still heard anger when she answered him.

"You damn well don't."

"How do you know?"

She tried to pull away, but he pushed her down and held her against her silk sheets.

"I love you, Clara."

"Sony's getting it anyway."

"I don't give a damn about the project, Clara. They can have it. I have others."

"I bet you do."

He lowered his mouth to hers and she held still for a long moment, but his lips worked on hers until she opened her mouth under his.

His mouth was warm against her ear as he whispered, "You can't shut me out, Clara."

"The hell I can't."

Fred laughed again, all tenderness gone from his eyes as if it had never been. He kissed her one last time and stood, moving to get dressed.

"We'll see."

5

PALM SPRINGS, 2010

CLARA WATCHED THE LIGHTS OF THE CHRISTMAS TREE FLICKER IN the soft gloom of the den. Her mother's antiques were hidden in the dark, indistinguishable shapes that seemed to loom around her, taunting her. The room was decorated in her mother's favorite tones of green and gold, but Clara could see nothing but darkness and the muted dark green carpet under her feet.

It was almost midnight on Christmas Eve, and household staff had gone home for the holiday. They wouldn't be back for two more days. Her mother and Darren were at a party at the country club, and Clara sat alone, listening to the silence.

For the first time in her life, silence wasn't a blessed companion, but a burden she wanted to set down. Earlier in the evening, she had watched television, but the emptiness of other people's holidays had soured her mood, and she had soon turned the television off. Next, she had listened to music, but rock and roll grated on her nerves, and Mozart made her think of her Aunt April, so she turned the music off.

Clara watched the colored bulbs cast their glow onto the twelve-foot ceiling above her head, and onto the Aubusson carpet at her feet. She wanted to go walking in the garden and out to the desert where she could wander for hours and never feel lonely. It was cold, though, and there was a full moon, so the lynx would be out, prowling.

She stood and paced across the thick softness of the Aubusson. The rug under her feet seemed to buoy and support her, though she knew the effect was an illusion and that there was hardwood underneath. Her mother had bought the carpet as a Christmas gift for herself two years before. A month later, she met Darren, and Clara's world changed.

She pushed thoughts of her mother and her mother's husband out of her head. She shoved them into a hidden room at the back of her mind and locked the door. It was Christmas, and she didn't want to think about Darren if she didn't have to.

Clara sat down on the soft rug, running her fingers across it. As a remnant of the time before Darren, it brought her comfort. Most of the house had been changed since his arrival, but like her, this carpet had survived. The softness under her hands reminded her of the last gift Aunt April had given her, the cashmere sweater Clara had never worn.

She brought the sweater out sometimes and looked at it. It was hidden in the bottom of a drawer, still wrapped in tissue paper. She would draw the box out slowly and unwrap the paper carefully so she wouldn't tear it. She would hold the sweater, still folded in her lap, and run her hand over it when she was feeling especially weak. Once, she had even leaned close to breathe in its scent. Her aunt's perfume still lingered, clinging to the folds of the cashmere.

When Clara caught herself doing that, she stopped taking the sweater out of its drawer, no matter how lonely she was. She hadn't looked at the sweater in over a year.

She lay looking up into the branches of the spruce her mother had ordered from the florist. Red and green were in fashion this year, and the entire tree was covered in nothing but red and greens balls, with red and green lights winking. Clara preferred the white and silver tree of the year before. The other had been cold, but this year's monstrosity hurt her eyes.

She remembered the Christmas before her mother's marriage,

the Christmas she had spent alone with her aunt in New York. Her uncle had been in Germany on business, and her mother had been with Darren in Cancun. Clara had arrived alone on a plane from Palm Springs, and her Aunt April had met her at the airport with a huge box tied with a green ribbon. Clara had opened the box while in the terminal and found a fur-lined coat and hat nestled in the tissue paper. April had known that Clara had nothing warm to wear, and that her mother, Jessica, hadn't given the cold any thought.

Wrapped in her mink-lined coat, Clara sat in the back of her aunt's limousine as they drove into the city from LaGuardia, breathing in the scent of leather and her uncle's cigar smoke. She watched the buildings of Manhattan rise before her as they crossed the Queensboro Bridge into the city.

April took her to the penthouse on Park Avenue. Though the city was just outside the glass of the windows, Clara couldn't hear the noise of the traffic as she stood looking down from her aunt's living room. The room was decorated in white, with white pillows and a white expanse of carpet that looked as if no one had ever stepped on it. Clara had hesitated before going in, and Aunt April laughed, wrapping an arm around her so they stepped onto the pristine carpet together.

Though it was the dead of winter, April's house was full of flowers, and Clara could smell the scent of roses and gladioli as she walked down the polished marble hallway to her bedroom. She had brought no dress pretty enough to wear for a formal evening in New York, but April had thought of that, too. A green silk dress was spread across the foot of Clara's bed, as if Clara herself had left it there, ready to slip on when she came home. She reached out and touched the silk reverently, and it slipped between her fingers like an eel. That dress was the first silk she'd ever worn.

April sent her maid to Clara's room before they went out, and the woman brushed Clara's hair until it gleamed. She drew the soft strands into an elaborate twist at the nape of her neck. When Clara saw herself in the gilt mirror, she smiled. She looked sixteen.

Her aunt had met her at the door to the elevator, a smile on her face. *"You're lovely, darling."*

Now, as she lay under her mother's Christmas tree, Clara could still feel the soft, cool brush of April's lips on her cheek.

That entire week in New York, Clara felt as if she'd fallen under an enchantment, and her aunt was the fairy that had drawn her into another world. Clara and April had dined alone in plush restaurants and gone to the theater every night, because April knew she loved it. One night, they went to Lincoln Center to hear Mozart's Requiem. Clara thought it was odd music to play at Christmas, but when she heard it, the haunting strains blocked out all thoughts of anything else.

Clara's favorite place in New York was the Metropolitan Museum of Art. She walked through the museum at her aunt's side, realizing that stood in a shrine built to honor people long dead. They moved slowly through the museum's collections, and Clara set the pace. April watched her niece as she drank in the sight of the relics of each civilization, one after another. Clara had never seen anything so old as the Egyptian temple that stood in a glass wing of its own.

They had tea in the café next to the sculpture garden, looking out onto Central Park. They could see the Egyptian obelisk, where it stood as a sentinel outside. Clara wanted to go outside to look at it more closely, but the rains were coming, so they stayed inside.

On Christmas Eve, they stayed home. All the staff had gone to be with their families, and Clara sat in front of the fire with her aunt, sipping hot cider lightly laced with cognac. The oak logs burned steadily, and they sat in silence, listening to the fire and watching the snow fall. It was early for snow. Aunt April had laughed and said she'd ordered it from Saks Fifth Avenue, just for Clara's benefit.

Clara fell asleep in front of the fire that night on the soft plush rug, with the touch of her aunt's hand on her hair.

She pulled herself out of her memories roughly, biting her lower lip. The pain of her lip distracted her from her thoughts, and she blinked. Tears escaped, sliding down her temples and into her hair, and she wiped them away.

Clara looked up at her mother's green and red Christmas tree with revulsion. She closed the flue of the fireplace to seal the dying fire behind its glass doors. Before she turned to go upstairs, she laid her hand on the switch that lit the tree. She hesitated for a moment before pressing it and enveloping herself in darkness.

The moon was full and high in the night sky. Moonlight filtered into the hallway from the conservatory. When Clara passed her favorite room, she didn't look to see the lawn and the desert beyond the glass as she usually did. She moved past the room on silent feet, climbing the curved staircase to her bedroom on the second floor.

Clara had come home from boarding school for the holidays against her better judgment. She wouldn't make the same mistake next year.

The empty house was as hollow as the belly of a whale, and Clara felt as if she floated alone on an empty sea. She listened to the echo as the grandfather clock in the foyer struck midnight.

6

PALM SPRINGS, 2010

THE NEXT MORNING, CLARA SLEPT LATE. WHEN SHE WOKE, THE SUN was already high over the desert, and the sprinklers were covering the lawn with a thin layer of moisture that would be absorbed by the grass and the dry air almost as soon as it fell. Clara lay in bed for a long moment, listening to the futility of the sprinklers running, and knew that without their constant motion, her mother's treasured lawns would burn to dust under the high sun.

Clara dressed in shorts, knowing the desert would be hot now that the sun had risen. She was careful to stay quiet as she moved down the front staircase, her mother and Darren still asleep. She went unnoticed as she slipped into the kitchen and filled her knapsack with bread, water and cheese. The kitchen was completely silent without Carol, the housekeeper, or Brenda, the cook, bustling through it. Clara felt a moment of superstitious fear that she had wandered into the wrong house, a house lacking their steady and reassuring presence. She left the kitchen as quickly as she could, moving silently in her tennis shoes so that she wouldn't break the spell.

She struck out across the lawns, watching the sprinkler system as it started watering the far eastern edge of the grass. She'd have to time her return so she could catch the sprinklers running along the back rim of the lawn. She would be hot later, and the cold water would feel good on her skin.

The air was warm already, and Clara sighed in pleasure as she crossed the edge of her mother's manicured lawn into the desert. The heat greeted her, and she felt as if she had walked through a wall into another world. Since it was December, it was only about eighty degrees. Clara was grateful for that. Being away at school for so many months of the year, she was no longer used to the desert heat. She stopped to take a sip of water before walking on.

She missed the desert most when she was at school in Colorado. She lived and studied on a mountain, and the aspens were green all year round, except when they were covered in snow. The town she lived in was designed to look like a Swiss village and had been built to support the girls' prep school she went to. The only people who lived in the town worked at the school in some capacity, and their families worked in the village, running fancy shops that sold chocolates and the latest New York fashions. The town was ideal for the nouveau riche families who left their girls at the school all year. With Aspen only twenty miles away, wealthy parents could spend a weekend skiing and see their daughters at the same time, thus assuaging their consciences before they moved on to Paris or the Amalfi coast, where their daughters knew they'd rather be.

Clara didn't mind the cold in Colorado as much as she'd thought she might. Even the snow had its own beauty when it was fresh and not yet trampled by the boots of teenage girls. She loved to take long hikes down the mountain trails, when the excess of feminine chatter and teenage minds was more than she could bear. Nothing could replace the desert in her soul, though, not even majestic mountains and deep blue skies. Even in summer, when the flowers were in bloom on the mountains and she felt as if Heidi might come bounding out of a hedge at any moment, Clara's longing for the desert was a physical pain.

She stopped for a moment to take in the sight of the desert in front of her, where it stretched towards the mountains in the distance. She sat on a rock that was already hot to the touch, careful not to burn her thighs. She knew she would be tan when she returned to school in a week, and everyone who hadn't gone to Biarritz for the holidays would be envious.

Clara uncapped her bottle of water and sipped it slowly, watching a hawk fly overhead on its way to the distant mountains. There was precious little to kill in the desert this time of day. All the animals, large and small, were smart enough to hide from the midday sun and heat. Clara smiled. She wasn't so smart. She was the only one left exposed.

She ate her bread and cheese, watching as the shadows began to creep ever so slightly to the east. She stood and stretched. As much as she wished she could disappear into the desert and never return, she knew she would not. She had hiked three miles, and she needed to start back. There was always the slight chance that her mother would be looking for her.

As she arched her back to release the last of her tension, she felt a chill on the back of her neck. The silence of the desert was broken by the sound of boots on rock. Her haven had been violated. Clara felt a surge of anger, which she quickly repressed.

She heard Darren's thoughts before she saw him, and she had trouble raising a mental wall against him. Surrounded by so much emptiness, she had allowed her mind to drift. There had never before been anyone in the desert to protect herself from.

She closed her mind, but not before she saw the flash of lust behind Darren's eyes which he was always careful to mask. He stopped six feet away from her and offered his boyish smile.

"Out for a hike, I see."

His perfect teeth gleamed in the desert sun, and his tanned face was lightly damp. Clara saw that he didn't have a water bottle with him, and without a word, she offered him hers.

"I didn't think I'd walk this far." He stepped toward her and took the bottle from her, his fingers brushing her hand.

Clara held herself still and forced herself not to back away. Darren drank deeply, and she watched the muscles of his throat move. He smiled, handing the water bottle back to her.

"You shouldn't hike out here without water," she said.

"So your mother's always telling me. I don't do it often. Guess I forgot."

He didn't move away from her but stood close for a long moment. She could feel his breath on her hair. Clara repressed another surge of anger, masking it as if he had the gift and could read her thoughts. She stepped around him deftly, sliding her water bottle into her knapsack. He brought himself out of his contemplation of her and offered the boyish grin that had won her mother's heart.

"Mind if I walk back with you?"

Clara swallowed the truth that rose to her lips. "No."

She moved back the way she had come. She saw nothing of the desert on their return, though the walk to the house was usually the most pleasant aspect of the trip, with the sun dazzling her eyes as it began to sink into the west. Darren walked in silence beside her until they were in sight of her mother's gardens.

"Well, that was nice," he said. "I always wondered where you disappear to when you come home."

In spite of her mental shields, Clara saw into his mind in that moment. He had seen her leave the house and had followed her. The brightness of the day seemed tarnished with that knowledge. She swallowed hard against the bile that rose in her throat.

"I don't go far."

He stopped and looked at her as they stepped onto her mother's lush lawn.

"No, I guess you don't."

She turned away from him, heading for the part of the lawn that was currently being watered. He didn't move to follow her but shaded his eyes against the setting sun.

"I'll see you at dinner, Clara."

She didn't answer, raising her hand in a half-hearted wave. The cold water of the sprinklers hit her, and she gasped. She felt the need to wash after spending an hour in his presence. She didn't look back but felt it when he went into the house. Once inside, he was too far away for her to read his thoughts. She had no way of knowing whether or not he continued to watch her from one of the downstairs windows. She didn't want to know.

Clara wore her new green silk dress to dinner that night. She had bought it in one of the fashionable shops in the village near her school. It was the kind of dress her aunt would have bought for her in a different world, the kind of dress to wear to the theatre in New York. The dress clung to her hips, and she smiled at her reflection in the full-length mirror. She wasn't going to hide herself because her stepfather was a lecherous bastard. Even at fourteen, Clara wasn't a woman to hide from anything.

As she came down the curved staircase, Clara heard her mother cursing in the kitchen. Jessica was trying to warm up the gourmet dinner Brenda had left for them, and it sounded as if her mother's attempt to turn on her own oven wasn't going well.

Clara stood in the hallway and heard Darren speak to Jessica in a soothing voice.

"Jess, don't worry about it. I'll call for a pizza."

She heard her mother's indistinct voice as she wept on her husband's shoulder. He gathered her into his arms and murmured to her softly so Clara couldn't hear what he said. She stood framed by the kitchen doorway, and Darren turned his gaze on her, meeting her stare over her mother's head. He saw her green dress, and Clara flinched as his gaze touched her. She wanted to go upstairs and take the dress off, but she wasn't one to retreat, even when she knew she had been defeated.

When Darren spoke, his voice sounded normal, the way any man would sound when speaking to a child.

"Well, kiddo, what do you want on your pizza?"

They sat in the dining room. Carol had set the table two days before, so all they had to do was lift napkins from china plates. Dust had settled in Clara's wine glass, and she brushed it out with her linen napkin. Darren filled her glass to the rim, and Jessica didn't comment.

Clara turned to look at her mother where she sat at the foot of the table. Her mother looked oddly fragile, her blue eyes wider than usual. Jessica didn't take her eyes off her husband, watching him as if he held the answers to all her questions. She was still upset about burning the dinner.

Darren was carefully attentive to her mother, even going so far as to feed her a bite of pizza from his own plate. His sweet attentiveness made Jessica laugh, and she lost the look of bewilderment that had filled her eyes after the burned coq au vin. Clara repressed a sigh. She was a stranger in her own house. Seeing her mother with Darren made her ever more aware of that.

Darren got a charge out of having her there. Clara could feel the sexual attraction roll off him in waves, though he sat at the other end of the table, next to her mother, crooning in her ear. He loved to lean close to Jessica, knowing that Clara was watching. Clara silently counted the days until she could get back to school. There were too many.

She was contemplating whether or not she should fly back a week early, when her mother's voice broke into her thoughts.

"Clara, honey, eat some more."

Clara smiled at her thoughtless mother, basking in her momentary attention.

"No, Mom. I'm full."

"Well," Jessica's eyes gleamed with childish glee. "We have a surprise for you."

Clara blinked. She hadn't gotten a Christmas gift from her mother in years. She watched as Darren brought in a big box tied with red and green ribbon.

"Not a puppy, I hope," Clara joked half-heartedly.

Jessica laughed, a sound like the tinkling of bells, as if Clara had made a witty remark.

"Open it and see."

Clara tried to ignore Darren's eyes trailing over her skin as she tore away the ribbon and paper that covered her present. She opened the box carefully, savoring the moment. She couldn't remember the last time her mother had given her a gift.

45

She pulled back the tissue paper and found a black nightgown nestled inside. It was beautiful, trimmed in delicate lace and beads of jet. It looked like something a thirty-five-year-old woman would wear, the gown of someone's mistress. Clara swallowed and kept her face scrupulously blank so she wouldn't reveal her pain. She knew Darren had bought the gift. Her mother had nothing to do with it.

Clara touched the silk nightgown gingerly before closing the box.

"Thank you." She took a deep breath before meeting Darren's gaze.

"I'm glad you like it, kiddo." He watched her, carefully, trying to gauge her reaction.

He couldn't tell what she thought of it, and he wondered.

"Well, give your father a kiss, sweetheart, and then give me one, too. We've got plans tonight, and we'll be out late." Jessica settled back in her chair, smiling.

Clara rose from her seat and moved to Darren. He lifted his face to meet her lips, but she kissed him on the forehead.

"Thank you, Darren."

"You're welcome."

She could see he was disappointed and that he wished they were alone. She frowned at his boldness. Clara realized that she was going to have to stay away completely.

She turned to her mother, and Jessica lifted her cheek for Clara's kiss. Jessica smelled of a sweet, light perfume, like the scent of summer rain on the trees in Colorado. Clara leaned close to her mother for a moment too long, but she couldn't force herself to pull away.

"Thank you, Mom."

"You're welcome, sweetheart. Merry Christmas."

Later that night, Clara climbed the staircase of the empty house, carrying her Christmas present. She laid the box on her bed and drew out the gown Darren had given her. She saw that it had been hand-sewn in France.

She took off her clothes and pulled the nightgown over her head. It fit perfectly, as if she'd been measured for it. She felt a chill, wondering how long he'd watched her, that he could have given her measurements so accurately to a seamstress she had never met.

Clara stripped the gown off in one quick motion and tossed it back into its box. She pulled on a flannel nightdress and hid the new gown in the bottom of a drawer, where she wouldn't have to look at it again.

She felt a creeping distaste slide over her skin, and a cold stone threatened to settle in her stomach. Clara forced herself to laugh so that the cold stone was dislodged before it could take hold. She would be damned if she'd let his sickness enter her mind and infect it like a cancer. She forced herself to make a joke, though she wasn't laughing.

Darren was a lecherous bastard who needed to die, but he had exquisite taste.

7

COLORADO, 2013

AT SIXTEEN, CLARA LAY IN BED, LOOKING INTO THE DARK. SHE could hear the girls around her, whispering. She would have sighed, but Clara knew she would be heard, so she swallowed it. She hadn't had a phone call from her mother in over a month, and when she called the house in Palm Springs, Darren and her mother were always out.

She had known what life would be like after her mother's marriage. Darren was always lurking in her mother's house, lying in wait for Clara. His constant presence was what had driven her away to boarding school in the first place. Though she had known what life would be like after her mother's honeymoon, foreknowledge hadn't made the reality any easier to live with. She resented having to flee her own home. For the last three years, she'd felt like a refugee.

There was always the possibility that Darren would die, killed by a blow to the head from some socialite's misdirected tennis ball. Clara hoped for that idly, the way one wished for rain in a desert, knowing it wouldn't come. She couldn't bring herself to wish him dead. Clara found that she was still too superstitious for that, though she had gotten over her fear of the dark when she was three.

Clara shared a room with a girl from England, who spoke with a drawling accent and carried herself like a queen. The girl's name was Clarice, and her parents called her once every week, though they lived five thousand miles away. She wondered why the girl had come to Colorado of all places for boarding school. Most wealthy Europeans sent their girls to school in Switzerland or France. Clara thought perhaps that Clarice wasn't bright enough to get into those schools, though money often paved over any such difficulties. Perhaps the girl was running from some demon of her own. Clara didn't look into her mind to find out, and she knew better than to ask.

Though she had lived with Clarice for two years, she knew almost nothing about her. After the first week, Clarice had given up her polite, guarded inquiries into the state of Clara's affairs, and had since not questioned her at all. Clara found the girl's presence soothing, her British reserve covering any faults she may have had, like her propensity to toss stockings over the radiators in their room.

Clarice had just returned from her month away with her parents in Nice, and now she lay next to Clara on the carpet. The girls in Clara's dormitory had decided that tonight, New Year's Eve, was the perfect time for a sleepover in the rec room. They were fresh from the holiday break, having been sent back to school so their parents could enjoy welcoming the New Year without restraint.

Clara had attempted to avoid the sleepover altogether, but the dorm mother had come to her and insisted that she be there. Since Clara had spent Christmas break at the school—on her own, for the most part—the dorm mother was certain that she needed some time with the other girls. Clara knew better than to argue with the diminutive woman. Mrs. Perlman was soft-spoken and always wore cardigan sweaters in pastel colors. Her soft tones covered a will of steel. She was the voice of authority in their dorm, and no one ever challenged her. Clara didn't consider a fight with Mrs. Perlman a battle worth winning.

She lay on her cashmere blankets, listening to Clarice snore lightly, and sighed. No one heard her, as the girls who were still awake chattered about the boys they wanted to sleep with. The girls who'd already had sex were doling out details to the girls who hadn't, as carefully as a pharmacist handed out pills. The knowledgeable girls hoarded their information with great care, and the other girls paid top dollar for it in deference and status.

Clara had status because she was a loner. She was as beautiful and as rich as any of the other girls at the school. Her mother's family was more famous than most, and the family money was about fifty years older. Clara kept to herself, by choice, so her company and interest were coveted prizes that most of the girls never won.

There were whispers behind Clara's back that she was a snob. Clara had always been able to hear the secret whispers of other people's thoughts. She wasn't surprised when people thought ill of her. People had evil thoughts most of the time. They thought evil of each other, of her, of people they didn't even know. Clara didn't take it personally that no one liked her. She knew they didn't like themselves, either. She could see into their minds, and she knew they held themselves in as much contempt as they held her.

Clara sighed again, and again no one heard. She wondered how much longer the chattering would continue, and when she might be able to sleep. It was three in the morning, and she had a chemistry exam the first day of the new quarter, which she hadn't studied for.

She was an indifferent student, not from a lack of intelligence, but from a lack of interest. Clara wasn't going to be a mathematician or a writer or a politician and had no need of the classes she took. She was careful to maintain a C-average, however. She didn't want to be forced to leave the school because of academic failure. The school was her haven, and she guarded it jealously.

The door to the hallway opened, and a streak of light fell across the plush carpet. Mrs. Perlman stood in the doorway, a sweater over her flannel nightgown. The girls fell silent, wondering if they were going to be forced to sleep.

Mrs. Perlman didn't censure them, however. She stepped into the room and stopped by Clara's bedding. She reached down and gently touched Clara's shoulder.

"Miss Daniels, may I see you for a moment?"

Clara felt the bottom fall out of her stomach. She stood and followed the woman into the hallway. Darren stood out there, hat in hand, shifting his weight and looking uneasy. He hadn't slept in a few days, and there were dark circles under his blue eyes.

Clara knew something was wrong with her mother, but she couldn't see any further into their thoughts. A wall of fear rose inside her, blocking their minds from her, and she was cut adrift. She stood looking at the slim fingers of Darren's hands as he clutched his hat. Mrs. Perlman touched her arm, and Clara forced herself to meet her gaze.

"Clara, your mother is very ill."

She swallowed and found her voice. "I know."

Mrs. Perlman didn't seem surprised by this admission but accepted it as sleepiness or confusion.

"Your stepfather has come to take you home."

Clara blinked to hear Darren described as being any relation to her, and the fog over her mind cleared. She looked into his thoughts then. Her mother had been ill for some time, and he hadn't told her.

She turned to Darren. "Do you have a plane waiting?"

"At the airport." He stated the obvious in his eternally inane way.

His gaze never left her face, except once, to slide over her body, seeking its contours under her heavy flannel gown. She felt her contempt for him rise in a wave of bile, and she swallowed it.

This bastard was her mother's next of kin and would make all medical decisions for Jessica. Clara felt the precariousness of that, coupled with sickening fear. She hoped her mother's doctor would tell her what was going on. If not, she would have to delve into Darren's mind, cesspool that it was, so she could find the answers she sought.

"I'll pack a bag." She heard her own voice, as calm as if it were that of another.

Mrs. Perlman touched her shoulder again, gently. "I'm sorry, Clara."

She looked into the woman's mind and saw that Jessica was

dying of cancer, the same cancer that had killed her grandfather years before.

Clara forced herself to speak. She made sure her voice was soft and kind, because Mrs. Perlman had always wished her well.

"Thank you."

She turned to walk to her room, and Darren moved to follow her.

"Do you need help?" His voice was coated with a sugared attempt at sympathy.

Clara wanted to strike him but held herself still until the impulse passed.

"No. I'll meet you downstairs in ten minutes."

"All right."

Darren watched her walk down the oak-paneled hallway until she disappeared around a corner. Only then did he turn back to Mrs. Perlman and begin to arrange for the rest of Clara's things to be shipped to California the next day.

She would not be coming back.

8

PALM SPRINGS, 2013

CLARA SAT IN THE HALLWAY OUTSIDE HER MOTHER'S BEDROOM. SHE could hear Carol weeping somewhere down the hall. Dr. Matthews stepped into the hallway and stopped by Clara's chair. She gripped the mahogany arms convulsively. Her face was a blank mask.

"I'm sorry, Clara."

She forced herself to meet his gaze. She could see his concern, and that it was a professional reaction, a part of his job. Still, it was the only genuine sympathy she was likely to receive. She took the hand he offered, grateful for his kindness.

"Thank you, Doctor."

The older man moved off down the hall, his footsteps whispers on the deep carpet. Clara watched his retreat and heard a new sound, the sound of Darren's thoughts as he stepped out of her mother's bedroom.

She turned to look at her mother's husband. He was only thirty-four and had been made a good deal richer by her mother's death. He hadn't loved Jessica, but he had sat by her side every day at the end, not leaving her even to sleep. In spite of what Clara knew of him, she respected that. Having access to the surface thoughts in his mind, and to occasional flashes of deeper thoughts, Clara was surprised to find that much honor in him.

Darren's face was haggard from a lack of sleep, and his tennis player's tan had faded. There were deep circles under his eyes, and his blue eyes were bloodshot. For a moment, Clara thought that he might actually shed a tear over her mother.

"Clara."

His voice was husky with exhaustion, and Clara tightened her grip again on the arms of her chair. She heard something else in his voice, and as she looked into his eyes, he reached out to touch her shoulder. He slid his hand down her back, caressing her in slow circles, as if to offer comfort. Clara stood up and stepped away from him. His hand dropped, and he simply stared at her, as if a glass door was locked between them, a door to which he held the key.

Clara moved past him into her mother's room. Darren came as far as the door, but as he watched her kneel by her mother's bedside, he had the sense not to follow her any further. He stepped discreetly back into the hall, where she knew he would stand waiting until she emerged again.

Clara touched her mother's face. Her skin had a grayish hue and was paper-thin under Clara's fingertips. She brushed her mother's hair back from her forehead, then stood and moved without thought to her mother's vanity table.

Jessica's makeup remained untouched on the table's glass surface. The maids dusted it every day and kept the little lamps on either side of the antique table polished to a high gleam. Clara selected the colors carefully, picking her mother's favorite blusher, foundation and powder, carrying them over to her mother's bed.

The housekeeper, Carol, came to stand in the doorway, wiping her eyes with a handkerchief. She watched as Clara knelt beside her mother and carefully began to apply makeup to her already hardening face.

She was skilled with cosmetics. It was the one thing her mother had taken the time to teach her. She remembered watching as a child while her mother applied each layer of paint, with reverence, as if performing a religious ritual. As Clara knelt by her mother's bedside and spread lipstick over her lips, she realized that the worship of her own beauty was the only religion her mother had ever practiced.

She felt tears in her eyes and let them fall as she smoothed a pearly gloss over her mother's reddened lips. She drew a brush through her mother's long blonde hair, the hair that the cancer hadn't managed to take as it had taken the rest of her beauty.

Clara laid her mother's pearl-handled brush down just as the ambulance arrived to take her mother to the morgue. She rose from her place at her mother's side, knowing that it was the last time she would see her. Her mother had ordered her own cremation months ago.

She looked down at her mother's face and remembered her as she'd been before Clara had gone away to school, before the cancer had taken her beauty. Jessica had smiled, and her blue eyes had held the promise that one day Clara would know all her secrets, that she had only to find the courage to ask.

Clara stepped away from her mother's bedside and let the ambulance attendants load her body onto a gurney. Her tears flowed freely, the tears she had never shed throughout her mother's illness, the tears she had never allowed her mother to see throughout her childhood, when Jessica was near, but occupied with other things.

Darren came and stood beside her, but he didn't touch her as she wept. The attendants carried her mother down the curving staircase to the marble foyer. Clara watched from the top of the stairs as they loaded her mother's body into the ambulance. They were gentle with Jessica, as if she were made of spun glass. They were careful not to jostle her gurney, though she could no longer feel pain. The red light on the roof of the ambulance flashed once in silence before it pulled away.

Carol wiped her eyes and closed the heavy front door. The only sound in the marble hallway was the sound of the grandfather clock striking midnight.

Darren cleared his throat, and Clara jumped at the sound. She'd forgotten he was standing there.

"You'd better get some sleep, Clara."

His hand lightly brushed her arm, and it warmed her skin through the thin silk of her blouse.

Clara stared at him for a moment before she nodded. "Yes."

She turned away from him and moved down the hallway to her bedroom., which was at the far end of the house from the suite that he and her mother had shared. Clara was grateful for that as she locked her heavy bedroom door behind her.

The lamp by her bedside was on, and her bed was turned down, the soft satin sheets gleaming in the dim light. Clara took in her familiar bedroom, surprised that it looked the same as it always had, now that her mother was dead. She'd expected the change to be reflected in her surroundings, for all she saw to be as gray as her heart was.

Clara saw the letter on the mahogany surface of her dressing table. She moved across the room and picked it up. She froze when she saw that it was from her aunt. She opened the envelope with numb fingers to find a birthday card with pink and yellow roses displayed on its front, a cheerful wish for her happiness inside. Aunt April always remembered her birthday, and her cards were always on time.

Clara opened a drawer in her dressing table and drew out a pack of matches. She lit one and held the flame against the card until it caught fire. The flame began to consume the paper, until she was forced to drop the card onto a silver tray. She watched as it turned to ashes, then as the ashes smoldered. When the ashes were cold and had turned the same shade of gray as her mother's face, Clara undressed for bed.

The funeral would be tomorrow afternoon. Her mother had always hated long waits.

9

PALM SPRINGS, 2013

Clara had bought a black silk dress months before so she would have something to wear to her mother's funeral. Jessica had been cremated in the early morning, and now Clara stood looking out over the desert behind her house, listening as a priest intoned a blessing on a body that wasn't there. Darren held the urn that contained her mother's ashes. At the appropriate time, Darren opened it and released her mother to the wind. The ashes scattered on the lifting breeze, swirling away towards the mountains in the distance. Clara didn't weep, but kept her face hidden under the veil of her hat.

None of her mother's tennis friends were there, only a couple of the members of house staff and Dr. Matthews. They all stood in a long moment of silence that was meant to be a time of prayer. Clara looked out over the desert that was her home, watching the sunset as it filtered through the gathering clouds, painting them brilliant hues of indigo and mauve.

She turned her head and caught Darren staring at her. He didn't smile, and she didn't look away.

~

Clara sat motionless in the deep leather of her mother's chair. There was a fire in the grate, since the desert nights were always cold. Darren stooped to add a log of hardwood to the fire. As Clara watched him, she found that she wanted to weep. Her mother had always tended the fire before she'd gotten sick.

"Clara."

Darren faced her, his back to the fireplace. His linen sports jacket was still unwrinkled, though the day had been long. Her mother's lawyer had just driven away after reading the will. The bulk of the estate had been left to Darren. A sizeable amount was held in trust for Clara, with Darren as trustee. Clara had almost laughed out loud when the will was read, but she hadn't wanted to shock her mother's lawyer.

Clara met Darren's gaze, but she couldn't read his eyes. His face was in shadow.

"Clara, I want you to know that I'll always take care of you."

Her smile was grim. "I don't think so, Darren."

He moved to the arm of her chair and knelt next to her on the thick Aubusson carpet. Her mother had chosen that carpet when Clara was ten. She remembered that while watching the play of light in Darren's eyes.

"I don't think you should go away to school anymore, Clara."

"I agree."

He smiled the boyish smile that had won her mother's heart. Clara could hear the wheels of his thoughts as they spun, calculating his next move. She felt his hand brush her knee, and then felt his palm press against her thigh. Still, he smiled, looking up at her in an almost beseeching way.

"I want you to stay here with me."

She swallowed the bile that rose in the back of her throat. "No, I don't think so."

She pushed his hand away and rose from the soft haven of her mother's chair. The black silk of her dress clung to her thighs as she stood. She heard the quiet sound of whispering silk as she moved across the room, away from him.

"Darren, I'm leaving."

He was on his feet and next to her in the space of a breath. His hands were on her arms, and she watched dispassionately as he turned on his boyish charm, the charm that had conquered her mother so easily. He drew her toward him until she was close enough to smell the brandy on his breath. She turned her face away so that his warm breath ruffled her hair.

"I know you're grieving. You're going to stay here so I can take care of you."

Darren's hands moved down her arms and around her to slide up her back. She could feel the warmth of his hands through the silk of her dress, and her stomach churned. But she hadn't eaten in two days, so she was safe from ruining her mother's carpet.

Darren didn't seem to feel her tension under his hands. Or if he felt it, he didn't care. Perhaps he was the kind of predator that fed on resistance. He watched her, his blue eyes hot with lust.

He must be sure of himself. He had never let her see his desire so openly before.

He launched into the beginning of a prepared speech, filled with lies.

"Clara, I love you—"

She couldn't stomach much more. "Darren, before you say anything else, we need to talk seriously." She drew away from him.

Surprised at the evenness of her tone, he let her go. "All right."

Clara moved back toward the fireplace. She felt his gaze on her as she moved. Now that there was some distance between them, she almost started laughing. He was ridiculous, with his false declarations. He must think her a fool. Of course, he had no idea she could read his thoughts and had read them since the day they met. At least her mother hadn't betrayed the family by telling him of their gift. Not that it was often a gift. But in this instance, as she played a game to secure her freedom and her life, the old curse served her well..

Clara turned on him and faced him squarely, grateful that she'd had enough sense to put the distance of a room between them. She suddenly had an almost uncontrollable desire to spit in his face.

"Darren, I know you want me. I know you've wanted me since

you met my mother. And as sick as that is, I have no comment on it."

He blinked. Slowly, the haze of desire cleared from his eyes. He stood looking at her as if he wasn't certain he'd heard her correctly.

"Now, I make no moral judgments about your preference for young girls. It's none of my business. I am sure, though, that Mrs. Harvell wouldn't share my liberal views."

Clara watched as he digested this information. His blue eyes darkened to indigo with fear at the mention of his latest lover's name.

"I know I'm not supposed to know about Mrs. Harvell. I do know about her, however. I know she's the next woman on your list. I know you plan to marry her as soon as you can without raising the eyebrows of your mutual friends. I know you've been fucking her and countless other women behind my mother's back since the day you met."

It must have been the clear, passionless tone of her voice and the absolute lack of expression on her face. He didn't protest or proclaim his innocence as she'd expected him to, nor did he attempt to use all the weapons of charm and sleaze at his disposal.

Instead, Darren sat down heavily on a straight-back chair that stood against one wall. Clara watched the blow of her words fall on him, and the look of helplessness that crossed his face. She searched his mind and found, to her surprise, that he was as bewildered as he looked, and that he was in pain. Clara was even more surprised to find that she pitied him as he sat forlorn in one of her grandmother's Hepplewhite chairs.

She took a step toward him, and he looked up, the expression in his eyes like that of a wounded puppy.

"I have a proposal which I think you'll find acceptable."

Clara pulled a chair across the room and sat five feet away from him, close enough that he could see her eyes, but far enough away that she could escape if he tried to touch her.

"You are going to set money aside for my personal use. Not much money, but enough. Ten million dollars will be enough to keep me until I come of age. This money will be unfettered in every way and will not be part of the rest of my trust, which will be turned over to me when I reach the age of twenty-one."

He looked at her. His voice was hoarse when he spoke. And she saw that in spite of his pain, he was willing to deal.

"And what will you do for me?"

"Well, for starters, I won't tell Mrs. Harvell about your interest in underage girls in general and in myself in particular."

Clara watched as he swallowed hard. He seemed to pale under his tan. He adjusted the tie at his throat. She wondered if she would have to bring to bear her knowledge of his other lovers, but she held back.

"Do we have a deal?"

Darren looked at her for a long time without saying a word. Then he stood slowly and crossed the five feet between them. Clara rose to face him, poised to dodge his hands, but he didn't try to touch her. There were tears in his eyes. For once, his eyes and his thoughts mirrored each other. With her mental shields down, Clara felt his pain like a blow.

"You hate me, don't you, Clara?"

She was shocked to feel tears rise in her eyes. In that moment, she was swamped by his pain, until she couldn't tell his pain from her own. All at once, she felt the loss of her mother like a vise on her chest, squeezing her breath away. She saw that, though Darren was a worthless human being, he wasn't a demon. And her mother had loved him. He was the only other person who had known her mother at all. Clara felt the sorrow of that, and a tear slid down her cheek.

Her voice was weak. "No, Darren. I don't hate you."

For the first time since she'd known him, he didn't seem like a monster. Suddenly, she saw him with the eyes of an adult instead of the eyes of a lost and lonely child. She felt her loathing for him drain away. Freed of that old loathing, she found herself empty.

He was just a man, out for what he could get. Many people were just like him. Many were worse. He was no monster. He was just a fool. It occurred to Clara that she might never know anyone but fools for the rest of her life. Time yawned before her like an abyss. She would always be alone in the gift that set her apart.

Clara felt her isolation crush her, the loneliness that she kept at bay most of the time through strength of will, focusing on other things. Years of solitude lay ahead of her. A long, straight road leading nowhere. She wept.

Her tears weren't the quiet ones she sometimes shed when she was alone. She sobbed, holding her stomach as if she might be able to stop, as if she might learn again to hold the sorrow in. But the dam had broken. Her pain mixed with grief for the loss of her mother, the woman who had loved her as much as she was capable of loving, but never enough.

Darren's arms went around her, and she flinched, for she wasn't used to being touched. But his arms were warm, and he wanted her. No one else ever had.

His hands were warm on her back as he caressed her, as if to comfort her. She started to pull away, but he wouldn't let her go.

"No, Clara, let me hold you."

She knew that the softness in his voice was a lie, that he felt nothing for her beyond lust. Now, though, she didn't care. Maybe that was all love was, a random physical coupling of strangers.

She saw something in Darren's eyes that made her feel the walls of her mother's house closing in on her. Loyalty and knowledge of another person were illusions. She would be alone all her life, as she had been alone since her Aunt April had left. And she wasn't the only one. Everyone faced the same truth. The only difference was that they accepted it, while Clara rebelled, wishing she wasn't alone, wishing for something that didn't exist.

She knew that if she fought him, he wouldn't let her go. She thought of the blows she might strike against his throat, against his groin, but she hesitated because she heard the bizarre turn of Darren's thoughts. He would have her on the floor, as he'd wanted her for years, and then he would give her the money she'd asked for. And not only the money, but everything else she wanted. He would sign away his guardianship and allow her to emancipate herself without a drawn-out legal battle. He would let her go without ever trying to see her again.

All this would happen if she let him do whatever he wanted to her.

She read his mind, as she'd read it since the day her mother had first brought him home. As always, she used it against him. Let him take her virginity there on her mother's living room floor.

Clara knew that after that day, she would never enter that house again. She might be alone in the world, but better alone and independent than trapped here for even one more hour.

She set aside all thoughts of violence and lay down on her mother's rug. Darren didn't question his good fortune but fell on her like a ravaging dog.

After it was over, Clara lay still, her breath slowly evening out. She had stopped crying. Her black dress was torn, but she knew after that night, she would never wear it again. She thought for one horrible moment that she might throw up, but there was nothing in her stomach to lose but bile.

Darren's weight was heavy across her body, pressing her down into the carpet. Expensive as the carpet had been, Clara knew she had rug burn on her shoulder blades. Just as she was certain that she couldn't bear one more moment of his touch, Darren lifted himself away and looked into her eyes. His hair was mussed for the first time since she'd known him. When he spoke, his voice was smug, as if his had been the victory.

"Clara, you have a deal."

10

MOJAVE DESERT, 2019

Donna stood in the shade of an awning, smoking a cigarette. She looked out over the desert suspiciously, as if she expected the ground to yield up a rattle snake at her feet. Donna always had the same look on her face every time she visited Clara on location. Whether in the forest, on a mountain, or by the seaside, she harbored a healthy dislike of the outdoors.

"Is this supposed to resemble Arabia?" Donna lifted a sardonic eyebrow over the rim of her Ray Bans.

Clara laughed, extending her hand so the makeup woman could finish touching up her fingernails.

"That's what they tell me."

Donna dropped her cigarette and stamped on it with the toe of her sandal.

"I don't think any of these people have been to Arabia."

"I doubt it."

The nail woman waved a hair drier over Clara's hand. Clara's assistant, Lila, handed her a chilled bottle of Evian.

Clara thanked her with a smile, grateful for the touch of the cool bottle. She sipped it carefully through a straw so she wouldn't smudge her lipstick.

"Sony has given the green light on the space trilogy Stan wants you to look at." Donna lit another cigarette.

The nail woman turned off the hair drier and left.

"What space trilogy is that?"

"You know. The one with the ray guns."

Clara laughed. "They all have ray guns, Donna."

"Well, this one has a lot of them. In the first film, you'd be a warrior princess leading a band of fighter pilots or something."

"It sounds like a *Star Wars* rip-off."

Donna snorted. "It probably is. But *Star Wars* sells, so a rip-off will, too."

"Is that their reasoning?"

Clara handed the empty Evian bottle to Lila, who quietly disappeared into the trailer.

"I don't know that they use reason. Do you want to look at the script?"

"As a favor to Stan for picking up this costume drama, I'll look at it. But no promises."

"Of course not." Donna pulled off her glasses to look Clara in the eye. "I thought you didn't do favors."

Clara shrugged. A woman from the wardrobe department came to puff out the sleeves of Clara's billowing dress. She was supposed to be a rich English woman, lost in the depths of the Arabian sands, rescued by a passing tribal chief. Basically, a rip-off of *The Sheik*, without the rape and the kidnapping element.

Clara stood and let the woman straighten the rest of her gown. She knew she looked like a giant meringue.

"I'm getting out of here." Donna put her glasses back on. "California sun murders my skin."

Lila stood silent, ready with an umbrella to escort Donna to her car.

"I'll messenger over the space drama script."

"I'll take a look at it."

"I'll see you when you get back."

With that, Clara's manager made her escape. As she strode away from the set, Donna looked down at each step her feet took, no doubt so she wouldn't step on any snakes. Clara's assistant followed Donna at a trot, keeping her shaded from the desert sun with a black umbrella stolen from catering.

That night, Clara stood on the terrace of the little hotel where the cast and crew were staying. The stars were thick across the night sky, and the desert air was cold on her skin. The silk of her dress was soft against her thighs as she strolled in lazy circles over the flagstones. No one came to speak to her. People on her movies always left her alone unless she called someone over. Clara found herself enjoying the silence.

She could hear the thoughts of the people drinking peacefully in the hotel bar. They sat at wicker tables, drinking frothy alcoholic drinks with little umbrellas in the glasses and fruit on the rim. Their thoughts were a quiet murmur, strangely relaxed for a crew this far into filming. The director was new and competent, and they were on schedule and under budget. Clara couldn't remember the last time that had been true on one of her films.

The director was a short blond boy fresh out of film school. He had a surprisingly good eye in spite of his training. And what would have been a banal rip-off of an old black and white film was turning into an honest love story. Clara felt even her performance improving under the direction of the blond boy. She fished in her mind for his name and found it. Charles. She liked to call him Chuck, to rattle him, but he never blinked.

She had toyed with the idea of sleeping with him but had abandoned it. Her performance was one of the best of her career, and it was due to him. Sleeping with him would ruin that.

Clara wasn't much of an actress and she knew it, but it pleased her to find that she was improving. She needed to remember this Charles and see to it that he was hired again.

She hadn't slept with anyone on this film, with the exception of a grip one night when she was especially tired. Sam had the body of a Greek Adonis. Clara had indulged herself and hadn't regretted it. As always, she had chosen well. Sam had been the soul of courtesy and had made no claims on her afterward.

Clara lit one of her cigarettes with her ivory-handled lighter. The flame warmed her hand briefly in the cool desert air, and she drew a long line of smoke into her lungs.

"That stuff will kill you."

She turned to smile at Fred. She hadn't even heard him approach. Not a murmur of his thought, not a whisper of his shoes on the flagstone terrace.

"You always manage to surprise me."

He smiled back. "That's why you keep me around."

"Do I?" She arched a delicate eyebrow at him. "Keep you around? I haven't seen you in three months."

Fred's smile widened. He seemed to admire her, even when she was rude. Clara basked in his approval. She was surprised at herself, because since her mother died, she'd never given a rat's ass what anyone thought.

She found herself relaxing even more, as she always did when she was with him. His presence soothed her even when she didn't need soothing.

"Well, you don't keep me around yet, but you will." His voice held no bravado, only confidence.

Clara laughed her throaty screen laugh, and a few grips drinking together inside turned their heads to listen. She nodded to them, feeling magnanimous. Fred always made her feel expansive, as if she could afford affability.

Clara breathed in her hashish smoke, then finished the cigarette and stubbed it out in a brass ashtray set into the marble railing of the terrace.

"What brings you into the wilderness?"

His blue eyes were warm as he smiled at her. "You."

"I'm flattered." She waited to hear what he would say next.

Fred didn't speak, however. He tilted his head back and looked up at the stars. The sky seemed infinite above the desert, more than the sky above the city. Clara didn't raise her head to look at the stars with him. Instead, she watched as he took a deep breath of the clean air and then sighed.

"I like the country better than the city." His voice was quiet, as if he were thinking out loud.

"Any country? Or the desert in particular?"

"Any country. Though this desert is beautiful."

"Not at noon it isn't."

Fred laughed, a flash of teeth white in the moonlight. She could see his cobalt blue eyes glint. They were so dark they looked almost black.

"I'll be long gone by then."

"Did you really drive all the way out here to see me?"

"Well, to give credit where it's due, I didn't do the driving. I came out here specifically to get you to sign a contract."

Clara laughed at that, her throaty laugh falling down into her belly. She laughed until tears came into her eyes, and she had to sit on the edge of the terrace railing to regain her breath.

"I'm sorry, Fred. I shouldn't laugh in your face. But that is rich."

He smiled at her pleasantly, unmoved by her amusement. He stepped away from her to a calfskin briefcase that stood like a sentinel a few feet away. He brought it over to the railing and propped it up on the marble, opening it with a flick of his wrist.

"Here's the contract. The light isn't very good out here, I know. But you can trust me."

Clara laughed more. She held her sides, feeling that she might split in two.

"Stop it, Fred. I'm going to lose my dinner."

He sat down next to her on the railing and extended the contract. "Just take a look at it. I'll send it to your lawyer in the morning."

Clara finally stopped laughing, wiping her eyes with her fingertips. "You really expect me to sign this?"

"Of course. It's a great film. *Blast Away* is the working title, but we'll change that during production. The studio wanted you signed for all three films, but I didn't think you should tie yourself down."

"You've got to be kidding me."

He looked at her blandly over the creamy pages in his hands. "Not at all. You'll be making double your usual salary, which I thought was quite generous."

"You're being generous to me?"

Clara listened to herself, expecting to hear fury in her own voice. But for some reason, she didn't get angry. She only felt mystified.

"Well, not me, the studio." Fred looked into her eyes. "I happen to know that Sony has approached you with a similar space trilogy. Our script is better, and we'll double your usual asking price. It's a great deal for you and for us. Willoughby wants you back, Clara."

She became still at the mention of Willoughby's name. "He should have thought of that before he passed on the costume drama."

"Oh, Clara, don't hold a grudge. It isn't like you."

"The hell it isn't. You don't know me very well."

She met his eyes again and found herself lost in their indigo depths. They were both silent for a long moment.

He spoke first, his voice gentle. "I think I know you better than most."

Clara waited for a stinging retort to come to her lips, for her hands to rip the contact in half and cast it back his face. Neither of those things happened. She simply sat, the cold marble of the railing under her legs, looking into his eyes.

"Double my usual salary, you say?"

A slow smile spread like a sunrise over Fred's face. His blue eyes had a clear light in them, almost as if he were proud of her.

"Double. Though of course, we can negotiate that upwards for the second film, once we have your signature for the first."

Clara looked at him for a long moment. "Do you have a pen?"

"What the hell were you thinking?" Donna's voice sounded strangled over Clara's cell phone.

Despite the terrible service in the desert, Clara didn't want to have this conversation on one of Sony's telephone lines.

"Did you just swear at me?" Clara smiled to herself, tapping her cigarette ash into a crystal ashtray.

She was sitting in her trailer with the air conditioning on full blast, waiting for Chuck the Blond to set up the next shot. Her assistant, Lila, sat quietly in a corner, doing a crossword puzzle.

"I'm sorry, Clara, but I'm in shock."

Clara listened over the line as Donna's assistant poured her a glass of bourbon. She bit her lip so that she wouldn't laugh.

"Clara, it just isn't like you to sign a contract before your lawyer has looked at it."

"You're right, Donna. It was damn foolish. What did Philip say about it?"

Donna sighed. "He said he's never seen such a favorable contract come out of a studio. He wants to know what you've got on them so he can use it, too."

Clara laughed. Lila rose from her corner and brought her a bottle of Evian and poured it over ice.

"Tell him I need to keep my dirt for future negotiations, but better luck next time."

"Well, it turned out fine. But Clara, promise me you won't do that again."

"Donna, you know that I don't make promises."

Clara heard Donna take a long swallow of bourbon. She relented in case her manager became too sloshed to finish looking over the contract.

"In the future, I'll be more cautious. This was a special case."

"Why is that?" Donna sounded intrigued at the possibility of new information, her drink momentarily forgotten.

"I can't go into it here, but we'll talk when I get back to town."

"All right. Just don't do anything else crazy, like run off to Hawaii before your PR tour, all right?"

Clara laughed her throaty laugh. "Put it out of your mind. Have I ever missed an opportunity to let the public adore me?"

Donna's snort was her only reply.

70

"I'll see you in two weeks."

"Really? The costume drama is going to wrap on time?" Despite her consummate professionalism, Donna could not keep the surprise out of her voice.

"It's all due to Chuck. He knows what he's doing."

Donna sounded mystified. "Fancy that."

11

LOS ANGELES, 2013

CLARA DROVE INTO LOS ANGELES FOR THE FIRST TIME AS THE SUN was setting. The traffic moved around her, but it wasn't rush hour, so her car kept a good pace. She watched as the buildings of downtown loomed before her. The hills that surrounded the city rose in the distance. She felt a pang for the sight of the desert and squelched it.

The rental agent had written down the address of her new apartment, a little studio in the Hollywood hills.

"*Slightly pricy,*" the real estate agent had said, eyeing Clara's fake driver's license with a raised eyebrow.

In spite of the look on the woman's face, Clara knew she passed easily for eighteen. She had paid a year's worth of rent in cash, so the agent hadn't been too choosy. She had read about her mother in *Vanity Fair* and had heard of all the money Clara's family had made in oil seventy years before. The woman hadn't asked any questions.

Clara walked into the apartment as the first stars of the evening were coming out. She could see very few past the bright lights of the city, but her deck faced the mountains, and the air that blew in her face was almost fresh. Clara smiled, leaving her suitcase on the deck while she turned to look at the rest of the house.

There was one long room, its hardwood floor stretching twenty feet in both directions. Clara found the closet, which was smaller than the maid's closet had been in her mother's house. In Darren's house, she corrected herself. He owned the house in Palm Springs now.

The kitchen was very clean and newly furnished with all the latest gadgets. The white tiles gleamed under Clara's feet as she opened every cabinet and peered into their cavernous emptiness. She stood looking at her little home in silence for a long time, reveling in the sound of quiet all around her. Her building was a converted house in a residential neighborhood. The sound of street traffic was far away.

Clara sat on the wooden floor of her empty apartment after bringing her suitcase inside. She plugged in her cell phone to charge it, placing it on a small tea table she'd brought from her bedroom in Palm Springs. It was the only thing, other than her clothes and a picture of her mother, that she had taken from that house.

She pulled on the sweater her Aunt April had given her on her twelfth birthday. The sleeves were too short and she could no longer button it, but wearing it gave her comfort. It was as if she could feel her aunt's arms around her again whenever she wore it.

Clara called a pizza place she'd noticed a few blocks away. She spent the first night in her new home eating pepperoni pizza on the floor, before she curled into her sleeping bag. She slept until the sunrise slanted through her six long-paned windows.

The next day, the gates of Barnett studios loomed in front of Clara. She had taken the bus to the studio so she wouldn't have to park her car.

Clara spent the morning eating a bagel and drinking endless cups of coffee at a sidewalk café, as she watched people move in and out of the studio gates. She listened to the surface of their thoughts, and smiled when she found the man who would get her inside.

He was short and harried, with a clipboard clutched in one

hand and a cigarette in the other. He was a second assistant director for a feature film, and he was late for that day's shoot. He had gotten drunk at a woman's house the night before, only to wake and find that his car wouldn't start. He now stood outside the studio gates, fumbling in his pockets for his pass.

Clara moved to stand next to him, taking his clipboard. "Hi. I'll hold that for you."

He grunted, looking at her suspiciously through narrowed eyes. "Do I know you?"

"Damn, Pete, I should hope you'd remember." She smiled at him, a slight smile, looking up at him through the corner of her eye. He shifted uneasily for half a moment, then decided to believe they'd slept together and that he'd forgotten.

"Oh, yeah. Hi, uh…"

"Clara. Clara Daniels." Clara kept her tone light and teasing with no hint of irritation.

Pete relaxed and smiled. He had found his pass.

"Are you here for the shoot?" he asked.

"No, I'm here to do their taxes."

Clara flashed him another smile, and he grinned back.

"Yeah, right." He flashed his pass and waved the guard away when she moved to follow him. "She's with *Flaming Arrows*. An extra."

The burly guard nodded and stepped aside.

"Where's your pass, Clara?" Pete dropped the stub of his cigarette and stamped it out underfoot.

Clara didn't miss a beat as she fell into step beside him. "They forgot to give it to me at the casting office yesterday."

She looked around surreptitiously so her curiosity wouldn't be noticed. She had never been on a studio lot before.

"Shit." Pete reached into his shoulder bag and drew out an extra's pass. "Pin this on."

Clara walked with him into one of the huge, barn-like studio buildings.

"Go check in over there, kid, and I'll see you later."

She smiled at him as he moved off, then stepped over to the extras' bullpen.

A woman took her name down on a pad and waved her inside.

"Did you bring a skirt?"

"No."

Clara didn't smile, because this woman, a woman named Phyllis, thought that smiles from extras were a liberty.

"Wardrobe will bring one." Phyllis waved her into the pen.

Clara took a seat on a metal folding chair and started to observe, her internal radar on full. She had a lot to learn.

Later that day, Clara found out later that she had snuck onto a costume drama. A wardrobe woman with two assistants came into the extra's bullpen, dresses and robes in hand. Clara slipped into a light blue gown that almost fit and that made her eyes look blue. She let her long hair fall past her shoulders, knowing the blonde strands showed up well against the sky blue of the dress. Once the wardrobe assistant moved on to the next actor, Clara adjusted the heavy belt around her waist so it fell at a more flattering angle. If her mother had taught her anything, she had taught her how to dress well, even without a mirror handy.

She was herded with the rest of the extras onto the set. The lights were so bright she squinted, but her eyes adjusted quickly. It was brighter than the desert at noon, and Clara smiled. She felt at home for the first time since her mother had died.

She looked around for Pete and found him talking urgently to the first assistant director. Pete was in charge of the extras and their placement, so Clara made sure she caught his eye again and smiled just enough to remind him they had a connection, but not in a cloying or annoying way. Unlike most of the people gathered there that day, Clara was playing the long game. If this particular show didn't help her move up, something else would. At sixteen, she had a lot of time to figure out how to work in this industry. In only five hours, she had already learned more than she'd hoped for.

Pete flushed a little and smiled back, a quick furtive smile, as if he didn't want anyone else to see him do it. Clara waited patiently. Then Pete called for her to come forward and placed her directly in front of the camera.

The first assistant director spoke to them all. "The king will be coming this way. When he comes in, I want everyone to bow or curtsey, OK? Most of you won't be in focus, but the few of you that are, I want you to look good, OK?"

Clara met his eyes and didn't smile. He also felt that smiling extras were too familiar. He nodded to her and she nodded back. She heard the wheels of his mind turn and watched him approach after consulting with Pete.

"Clara. Is your name Clara?"

Clara did smile then, but only a slight smile of acknowledgment. "Yes."

"When the camera pans around, I want you to curtsey deeply. The king is going to notice you and stop. Stay down until he brings you back to your feet. When he says his line, something like, *Good evening, madam*, or some crap like that, say, *Thank you, my liege*. OK?"

"OK."

The director strode onto the set, and the first AD moved away. Clara would have known the director even if she hadn't been telepathic, because an entourage of designers followed at his heels. He took in the entire set with a quick glance, and then spoke to the first AD who was suddenly at his elbow.

The first AD nodded, and then called, "All right, people, stand by. We want to get this right on the first try."

Clara turned as she had been told, and curtseyed as the lead actor swept in. He stopped in front of her, as they'd said he would, and raised her to her feet.

"The ladies at court become ever more charming."

She looked up at him through her eye lashes and smiled, having decided that her character was a courtesan and a secret favorite of the king.

"I thank you, my liege."

The King moved on, and once he was off camera, the director

called, "Cut."

The first AD frowned. "Was that the line?"

Clara didn't move but waited for the judgment of the director. He paused for a long moment, and everyone around him waited to see what he would say. Clara almost laughed as he drew out the moment for dramatic effect, thinking that a camera should be rolling to capture it. He spoke to no one in particular, as if pronouncing a judgment of deep insight and import.

"The new line is better. Keep it."

"Keep it," the first AD called in Clara's general direction.

Pete moved to her side and spoke low, as if she hadn't heard the last two statements.

"Keep the line the way you said it, Clara."

She nodded as if she took the entire farce seriously. "All right."

"Reset!" the first AD called, and there was a flurry of motion.

Clara took a deep breath so she would not laugh out loud. If these were the people she would have to manipulate in order to become a star, she would have no difficulty.

The camera started rolling again, and Clara sank into a deep curtsey. The scene was done fifteen times before the director was satisfied, and at the end of the process he nodded to her once, curtly, before stalking off. Clara raised an eyebrow, surprised that he would acknowledge her at all, but said nothing as Pete came to stand at her elbow.

"Clara, you did great. I think the big boss will want you for another throw-away line tomorrow. Just come this way, and we'll fill out the paperwork."

"All right." Clara fell into step beside him, careful to hold her skirts high so she could step over the cables that covered the floor. "What paperwork, Pete?"

"Come on, you're no greenhorn." Pete grinned, looking at her sideways. "You know you've got to sign for your pay increase. You're SAG eligible now. You'll need to sign for that, too."

Clara smiled. "I was just testing you."

He laughed, and she made a mental note to find out what SAG was, and if it was a club, whether or not it would benefit her to join.

12

NEW YORK CITY, 2019

THE LONG GREY LIMOUSINE WAS STUCK IN TRAFFIC ON 9TH AVENUE. Clara had gone shopping, and now it looked as if she might be late for the taping of the Steve Stimmerman Show. She thought Steve was a prick, so she didn't care if her tardiness made his life harder.

In the seat in front of Clara, Donna was sucking down her second glass of bourbon, talking into her cell. She was arranging the next day's spot on the *Patsy Jo & Renaldo Show*. Clara didn't think it was a good idea, but Donna insisted that the women who watched *Patsy Jo* would also watch *Desert Drift*. They were the women who kept the paperback romance industry afloat. They were a huge market, so Clara was going to get up at 6:00 a.m. the next morning to court them.

Donna hung up with the people at ABC and grinned. "They say Steve is shitting a brick."

"And how is that unusual?"

Donna snorted, swirling the last of her bourbon in the bottom of her glass. "I just wish I was there to see it."

Clara touched-up her lipstick, studying her reflection in her pocket mirror. Her eyes were incredibly green today, most likely because New York was so grey. She shivered, pulling her cashmere sweater closer around her body. She missed the desert.

They made it to ABC half an hour before the taping. Clara could see a line queuing around the front of the building.

"Haven't those people been seated yet?" she asked.

"The ones getting in have. Those are the people hoping to catch a glimpse of you as you go in."

"Don't they know that we pull in at the back?"

"Evidently not."

Clara smiled. "Let's give them a show."

"What?"

She leaned over and hit the intercom button so the driver could hear her through the dark glass between the seats.

"Hi. Ron?"

"Yes, Miss Daniels."

"Pull up out here."

"In front of the building, ma'am?"

"Yes. That'll be fine."

"Yes, ma'am."

She sighed, leaning back against the deep leather of her seat. "I love obedient servants."

"Clara, I don't think this is a good idea." Donna swallowed hard, looking out the tinted windows at the crowd gathered outside.

As soon as they saw the limousine come to a stop, they turned, jockeying for position to see who might get out.

"Sure, it's a good idea. Those aren't press. They're my public." Clara smiled, her adrenalin flowing.

She lived for moments like this. This was the reason she'd chosen showbusiness over any other career. Adoration was something she craved, like air and water. Adoration from a mass of people who didn't know her and would never know her. Adoration from people who only knew her name and repeated it like a mantra or a prayer. Clara liked being someone else's prayer.

She didn't wait for the driver to come around to open her door. She opened it herself and stepped out, smiling. The people around the car gasped when they saw her, and then started talking excitedly all at once.

"Is it her?"

"Oh, my God. It's Clara Daniels."

"She's much prettier in person."

"Look at her hair."

"Look at those diamonds."

Clara assumed that comment was directed at her earrings, which she thought were fairly modest. She stood still and let them look. The crowd left a wide berth around her, and Donna came around from the other side of the car, adjusting the tight skirt of her suit as she hurried. Clara slammed the limousine door and moved into the crowd.

"Hi," she greeted one of the women, who stood still and didn't speak or smile back.

The woman only stared at her as if she were a goddess come down to earth.

Clara moved forward slowly, and the crowd parted for her, jostling each other to get a good view of her. There was more than one tourist in the crowd, and camera phones were raised. Clara stopped and smiled for the people with phones, so more pulled them out.

"Miss Daniels, would you take a picture with my mother?" The little woman looked up at her, blinking as if she stood in a bright light.

Clara smiled at her personally and spoke in her lowest, most melodious voice.

"I'd be happy to."

She stood for pictures with several different people before she moved on into the building. Unlike the press, these people gave way before her. She gave a few autographs as well, smiling all the while. She fed off their energy as a vampire feeds on blood, and when she walked inside the building, she was high on it.

"Donna, that was amazing!" Clara took her manager's arm and drew her toward the elevator.

Security held the door for her as they stepped into the wire mesh cage, and Clara gave him a dazzling smile. He blinked and said nothing. She could see he didn't know what to say, and she felt a greater rush of triumph at conquering him, because she knew he saw celebrities every day, and that she was something special.

Donna pulled out her asthma inhaler and drew in a deep breath of spray. "Dear God, Clara. What if one of those people had a gun?"

Clara chuckled, her throaty laugh filling the elevator box. "Then they would have handed it to me and asked me to take a picture standing with it."

Her adrenalin flowed hot in her veins, and she knew she was flushed as if from a run.

The Stimmerman producer was waiting for them as they stepped off the elevator.

"So, you ladies took the scenic route, I hear."

He smiled, but Clara was not fooled. She could hear the contempt in his thoughts.

"Donna, find Rich for me, will you?"

Clara moved down the narrow corridor without sparing the producer a second glance. Donna went in search of Richard Smithson, the executive producer. The man who'd met them at the door stood alone in silence, his mouth opening and closing like a fish.

Clara was in makeup when Rich found her. He knocked on the door before coming in, as if she were his maiden aunt. She laughed at him, and he looked sheepish. He was the most boyish man she'd ever slept with.

"Hi, Rich. Sorry we're late."

"No problem, Clara."

She raised an eyebrow at him as the makeup woman powdered down her cheeks.

"Well," Rich grinned, "not your problem, anyway."

Clara laughed again and watched as Rich relaxed against the doorjamb. She met his blue- eyed gaze in the mirror.

"So, I hear you've gone back with Barnett Studios."

"Temporarily anyway."

"It sounds like they should have taken a harder look at *Desert Drift*."

"Who says so?" Clara's voice was noncommittal.

"Everybody. The preview screenings went through the roof. Those women love a good love story."

"Well, if the film's any good, it's because of Chuck. God knows the script was crap."

"Off the record, of course." Rich winked at her.

"Of course."

"Who's Chuck?"

"He's the kid director they hired out of USC to do the film. You guys should have him on the show. He's great."

"Oh, really?"

She could hear the suggestiveness in his voice. She would have known what he was thinking even if she hadn't been a telepath. She chose to ignore the innuendo.

"Really, Rich. He even made me look like I can act, and we both know what bullshit that is."

"We're ready in five," called a production assistant, running down the hall.

"Thanks." Rich nodded to the girl as she passed. "It looks like you're on, kid."

"I'd better get to the green room, then."

She stood after letting the makeup woman pull the towel from around her neck.

Clara nodded to her. "Thanks, Denise."

The woman smiled suddenly, as if lit with an inner fire. She was shocked that Clara had remembered her name.

"You're welcome, Miss Daniels."

The red light on the camera went off, signaling a commercial break.

Clara leaned over to sip her water, checking her microphone as she did so. Steve smiled at her, and she braced herself for his next comment. She had effectively blocked out his thoughts. They were such a cesspool, she didn't want to see what was coming next.

"So, who've you been humping lately, Clara?"

She smiled at him, stretching like a cat. "No one you know."

"You never know. You get around. How about Manley Steinbeck? You done him yet?"

Clara sipped her water meditatively, as if she were considering his question.

"Well, Steve, you know he's never been the same after having you."

The stage manager called out, "Five seconds!"

The girl counted out the rest of the time on her fingers, and the red light went back on.

Steve gave her his boyish grin. "Clara, I'm really happy you could stay for an extra
segment."

She flashed her one-thousand-watt smile and turned her head slightly so the camera could pick up her best angle. She included the audience in her warmth, drawing them deeper into the circle of her light.

"Steve, you know I always love spending time with you."

Clara left at last, making way for the Flying Tansy Twins, who were trapeze artists and ventriloquists.

"Steve's really hurting for guests today," Clara said to Donna.

She stood still as a production assistant from the sound department unstrapped her mike. She smiled at him, and he floundered a moment before he managed to smile back.

Rich met her in the hallway and kissed her. He fell into step beside her, and they walked toward the elevator in companionable silence, Donna trailing behind them. They were moving past the green room when a man stepped out and extended his hand to Clara.

Rich started to step between them, but Clara simply smiled. She'd already glanced into the man's mind earlier that afternoon. They had nearly run into each other outside makeup. She already knew what he was going to say, and she knew he would be good for a laugh.

"Hi, Clara. I'm Will Quigley. May I call you Clara?"

The man's eyes gleamed manically, his bangs sticking up from his forehead. Clara noticed he had moussed them so they would stay raised, like a porcupine's quills.

Rich fidgeted beside her, but Clara kept smiling. Donna took a deep breath, then reached into her bag for her asthma spray. She'd seen Clara smile just that way at a mugger before she broke his collarbone.

Clara's voice was serene. "That all depends, Will."

The man plowed on, like the salesman he was. "Clara, I represent a men's organization called the MFPP, and I was wondering if I might have a moment of your time."

Rich opened his mouth to tell the guy to back off, but Clara laid a restraining hand on his arm.

"You have a few seconds before I start walking to the elevator. Go ahead."

The man's grin was so big it threatened to split his face. "Great! My organization is Men For Porn Power, or MFPP. We're a group dedicated to the continuation and support of soft core pornography all over this great U.S. of A."

Clara swallowed her laughter as Donna reached into her bag and drew out a flask of bourbon.

"How interesting."

"We're asking for your support at our national convention this week at Madison Square Garden. We'd be honored if you could attend and possibly give a short speech on pornography and how it relates to your life as a film star and celebrity."

"But I don't do porn, Will."

Rich started smiling. He hadn't seen Clara play cat and mouse in years, and he leaned back, arms folded across his chest, and watched her. He couldn't let her savage the guy too badly, since he was the next guest on the show after the Flying Tansy Twins. He stood ready to hustle Clara quickly down the hall before she drew blood.

Will was undeterred by Clara's lack of enthusiasm. "Clara, if you don't do porn, it's because you don't understand it. Our American porn industry gives work to hundreds, even thousands, of aspiring filmmakers every year. And the foreign sales alone—"

Clara started to move forward, and Rich breathed a sigh of relief. He wasn't going to have to rescue the man, after all. Clara was going to let him slip the line. "That's very informative, Will," she said. "I'm still not interested."

The little man followed at her heels. Donna drew back from him, careful to keep her bag from brushing his shoulder in the corridor, as if he were diseased and it might be catching.

Will, lover of porn, kept talking. "But Clara, soft core porn has everything you can ask from a film genre. It has inventiveness, catharsis, athletic prowess. There's nothing you can't draw from it."

Clara stopped in mid-step. She saw a production assistant bearing down on them grimly, coming to collect Porn Will for the next segment.

She dropped her voice to a confidential tone. "William, I tell you. You've made me see the light."

Porn Guy beamed. Donna cast a startled look at Clara and started hyperventilating.

"When I decide to start stripping in public, Men For Porn Power will be the first to know. Until that auspicious day, let me give you a little advice."

Will leaned closer to hear Clara as she lowered her voice even further.

"I happen to know that Steve Stimmerman is the man you're looking for. Not only will he give a speech at your convention, I have it on good authority that he wants to join your group."

Rich started to groan, but Donna kicked him. Porn Will didn't notice this exchange. His glowing eyes were only for Clara, and they lit up as if he were one of the Chosen and he had seen the Second Coming. He stood in breathless silence as Clara passed him.

She landed one parting jibe over her shoulder as the production assistant came to lead Will away.

"Ask him on the air, Will. He'll be thrilled."

Rich's voice was low. "Clara…"

She ignored him, sending one of her one-thousand-watt smiles to Porn Guy. He looked back in awe at her as he was gently led away.

"I'll do that, Clara. God bless you."

She waved one hand to him in a casual salute, as Rich leaned over to whisper in her ear.

"Steve is going to shit a brick."

Clara kissed his cheek, smoothing his tie as she did. "Then that'll be the second time today."

Rich laughed under his breath. "I'll see you later, Clara."

"I hope so, Rich. Watch your back. Steve's feisty this afternoon, and now he'll be worse."

He laughed. "Nothing you couldn't handle."

"Never worry about me."

Later, in the car, Donna answered her phone. Clara rested her head against the leather seat, drawing smoke into her lungs from her hashish cigarette.

Steve's show had been a triumph. She loved rubbing his face in the fact that she was more popular than he was. Ever since she had refused to sleep with him two years before, she'd been a favorite target of his witless comments.

Donna's eyes were wide as she listened to whomever was on the other end of the phone line.

"Hold on a minute." Donna cupped her hand over the receiver. "Clara, it's for you."

"No kidding." Clara reached over and took the phone.

"Clara, wait—"

"Hello."

"Hello, Clara." It was Aunt April's voice.

Clara choked on cigarette smoke for the first time since she was twelve years old. She put out the cigarette in one of the limo's ash trays, while Donna reached over and pounded on her back. Clara shot her a glare, and Donna stopped pounding. She poured a glass of water instead and handed it to her.

"Clara, are you all right?" April asked.

She blinked away tears and took a breath.

"I'm fine." Her voice was hoarse, and she took a drink of water.

April sounded just as she had the last time Clara had seen her. The silence on the phone line lengthened. It had been ten years since Clara had last heard April's voice.

"I understand you're in New York," April said.

"How did you get this number?"

April paused for the barest moment. "I really don't think that's important. Do you?"

Clara's uncle had a lot of money and knew everyone on both coasts. His people could get anyone's number, given twenty-four hours to do it.

"No, I suppose not."

"I want to see you, Clara."

"I don't think that's possible."

There was a long silence. She heard her aunt draw a ragged breath.

"Clara —"

She couldn't read her aunt's mind, but she could hear the pain in her voice. Ten years of resolve crumbled in the space of a breath.

"When?"

She heard April lay the phone down for a moment, and another silence stretched, broken only by the sound of tissue rustling. April picked the phone back up, and her voice was thick with tears.

"Tonight."

"Do you still live on Park and 86th?"

Clara felt as if she were watching herself from a distance. She almost couldn't feel the phone in her hand.

April's voice was even when she spoke again. "I'll see you at seven."

Clara didn't even glance at her watch. "I'll be there."

Donna took the phone back, her eyes wide. It was after six-thirty. They didn't speak to each other, but Donna turned on the intercom and directed the driver uptown.

13

NEW YORK CITY, 2019

CLARA STOOD IN THE MARBLE HALLWAY OUTSIDE APRIL'S DOOR. SHE heard the bell chime inside her aunt's apartment, distantly, like a call to prayer. After only a moment, a woman in a starched black dress opened the door. Clara stood in silence, blinking at her. She couldn't find her voice.

The woman spoke for her, her voice low and melodious, more like that of an opera singer than a servant.

"Please come in, Miss Daniels."

The foyer of her aunt's penthouse was paneled in mahogany, and the mahogany floor gleamed. Soft light came from electric sconces along the wall, and flowers stood a table in front of the door, giving off the sweet scent of hyacinths and gladioli. The maid took Clara's coat, drawing it from her body and folding it carefully over one arm as if it were priceless. The woman could see Clara was in shock, and she spoke gently to draw her out of her stupor.

"Please come this way."

Clara followed mutely down the hallway from the foyer to a wide door that opened into her aunt's sunken living room. White carpet stretched in an almost endless expanse. Clara wondered if she bent down to touch the carpet's whiteness, if it would come off on her hand. She knew then that her mind was wandering, and she forced herself to raise her gaze from the floor, to look at her aunt for the first time in ten years.

Aunt April stood by the fireplace against the far wall, wearing a cobalt blue gown. The silk caught the light from the fire, and the color seemed to shift as she moved, so one moment the folds of the gown shimmered cobalt, the next moment a deep indigo, the next a light blue-gray. Clara lost her breath as her aunt turned to face her. In the years that stretched between them, she had forgotten how much April looked like her mother.

The silence seemed endless, and Clara found that she couldn't bear to let it continue. She knew she was wearing her heart on the planes of her face, and she schooled her mouth into the lines of indifference, the hard-earned indifference she'd learned during the years Darren had lived in her mother's house.

"I didn't dress for dinner." Clara forced herself to speak, and found that her voice was steady, almost cool.

She looked down and away from her aunt, smoothing the front of her faded jeans, drawing her cashmere sweater tightly around her shoulders.

When she looked up again, she avoided the sight of Aunt April, and instead looked over her shoulder at the mantel behind her. There Clara saw a photograph of herself in a silver frame. A recent photo, taken at the *Shout!* premiere. Nick wasn't in the picture. Clara was looking over one shoulder, laughing. She wanted to know which photographer her aunt had bribed to get it, but she didn't ask.

April met her gaze, unblinking. Clara saw that her aunt had been crying, and her first instinct was to move to her side and offer comfort, as April had always comforted her when she was a child. Before she took a step forward, Clara remembered vividly the first lonely days after her mother's marriage to Darren, how she'd waited in vain for even a phone call from her aunt, and how no call had ever come. Remembering this, Clara found herself thrust back for a moment into the horror of those painful days, during the first year of April's desertion. Clara didn't move to comfort her aunt but stood watching her in silence.

April crossed the room to stand just a few feet away from her sister's daughter. Her ash blonde hair was swept up in the twist that Clara remembered from her childhood. Diamonds and sapphires winked at her ears, catching the light from the lamp on a nearby table, transforming that light into prisms of fire. April's voice was just as Clara remembered it—soft, just as she always heard it in her dreams just before she woke.

"I'm sorry I didn't come to the funeral," April said.

"We didn't expect you."

"No, I suppose you didn't."

April reached out as if to touch Clara's arm, but stopped mid-motion. She drew her hand to her own hair instead and fiddled with the sapphire in her earring.

"Would you like a drink?"

"A vodka and soda, no ice."

April nodded to the maid, who moved to a bar at the other end of the room. The mahogany bar stood by a window that led out onto the balcony. Central Park lay below, and the skyline of New York. Clara didn't look at the view. She kept her eyes on April's face.

She accepted the glass the maid handed her.

"Thank you, Mary. That'll be all." Her aunt's smooth voice didn't betray any of the emotion that Clara could see simmering under the surface of her composure. She still knew April well enough to see the tension in her hand as she fiddled with her earring for the third time in two minutes.

The maid was silent as she walked away. Clara found herself wondering, as she always did, where good servants learned that quality of silent motion.

April faced her niece then, not flinching from her gaze. "You look beautiful, Clara."

"Thank you."

Clara moved to sit on one of the plush white sofas that faced each other in the center of the room. April moved with her and sat on the opposite sofa. Somewhere deep within the penthouse, a clock chimed seven.

"I'm early," Clara said.

"I'm glad."

She looked away from her aunt, raising her drink to her lips. The liquor burned as it hit her tongue, spreading a pattern of warmth as it slid down her throat. She swallowed twice, her eyes not leaving the white carpet under her feet.

"How are you?" April's tone was deceptively calm.

Clara met her gaze and felt tears rise. She blinked them away before she spoke, wondering if her aunt had seen them. Clara's eyes didn't seem to realize that she had stopped mourning this woman years ago.

"Why did you ask me to come here?"

"I wanted to see you."

"Why?" Clara took another burning sip of vodka.

April looked away and took a deep breath. As always, her aunt's mind was closed to her, but Clara could see the pain in her face. Her aunt reached again for her sapphire earring but stopped herself before she touched it. She watched her aunt's battle to place her hands in her lap and leave them there.

"I tried to call you at home and at the studio," April said. "I was never put through."

"I told them I wouldn't accept your calls."

Clara knew herself to be a hard woman, but she rarely thought of herself as cruel. She did now, as she looked at her aunt's crumbling face.

"You accepted my call today."

"That was an accident."

There was a long silence. April sat motionless across from her. Clara could see that she had hurt her again. She didn't want to hurt her aunt, but she couldn't seem to stop herself.

April's voice was soft, almost a whisper. "I miss you."

Clara took a sharp breath. "Don't."

"Don't what? Tell you that you're my only living family? That I love you? That I'm sorry?"

April's voice shook, and Clara found that she couldn't take her eyes off her aunt's face, though she desperately wanted to. She wanted to deny the pain in April's voice and the pain in her own heart, but there it was, as crushing as a vise that wouldn't loosen its grip.

Clara felt a tear run down her cheek. April kept speaking, and Clara could see it was an act of courage, not bravado. Her aunt hadn't planned to speak so plainly, but now she couldn't stop herself. Clara listened as the words flowed unchecked, like the torrent of a swollen river.

"I do love you. I am sorry. I regret that I let that bastard run me off when you needed me. I'm sorry that I was weak. That I am weak."

April stopped speaking, and Clara looked down. Tears clouded her vision, making the white carpet blur.

When April spoke again, her voice was devoid of pain. It held resignation, and the realization that the damage couldn't be undone.

"I know what I did is unforgivable. I'm not asking for forgiveness. I only wanted to see you again."

Clara's tears kept falling. She didn't wipe them away. She didn't look up, but sat in silence, listening to April's soft voice.

"Are you happy, Clara? I know I don't have the right to ask that, to ask anything of you. But tell me anyway."

Clara laughed at that, startled, her throat thick with tears. She had no handbag to pull a Kleenex from, no servant at her elbow to offer her one. She used the back of her hand to wipe her nose, the way she had when she was a child, before she had learned restraint.

"You want to know if I'm happy?"

"Yes." April sat poised on the edge of the sofa, her drink untouched on the table in front of her, her eyes riveted on Clara's face.

Clara sniffled, taking a sip of her vodka. "I don't know that I've ever been happy. I've got what I want."

"And what's that?"

Clara opened her mouth to speak of her career, of her attempts at acting, of her adoring public. She found that no sound would come. She closed her mouth and swallowed convulsively.

"Are you in love?" April asked.

Clara blinked at the abruptness of the question, at the desperate way her aunt seemed to wait for her answer.

Clara found herself considering the question seriously. She didn't laugh it off as she would have if anyone else had asked it. She looked into her own mind and found that she couldn't lie to herself about this anymore than she could lie to herself about anything.

She took a deep breath, searching the feelings that she spent most of her life denying she had. Her aunt's question brought an emotion to the surface of her thoughts that had been buried deep and jealously guarded.

Clara was surprised to discover within herself a tiny flame of secret passion that she'd been harboring without knowing it. She wanted to squelch it. She wasn't a woman given to romantic leanings of any kind. Love wasn't a word in her vocabulary any longer.

Then Clara looked into her aunt's face and saw love for her shining in her eyes, mingled with pain. April was waiting patiently for an answer. Clara told her the truth.

"I love a man. His name is Fred."

"Does he love you?"

Clara didn't have to search for this answer. It came to her lips almost before she had a chance to form the word in her mind.

"Yes."

April smiled then, a sheen of tears in her eyes. "I'm glad."

Clara smiled back, and for the first time looked at her aunt without a stab of pain. The older woman reached across the glass table to take Clara's hand. She did not pull away.

14

LOS ANGELES, 2015

THE AIR IN THE TRAILER WAS STALE. THE AIR CONDITIONER WAS working overtime against the July heat. Clara shifted in her folding chair. Though the air was cool, she still felt like she was suffocating.

Clara ordered herself to stop complaining, even in her own thoughts. She was studying film making, and this stifling trailer was part of her apprenticeship.

Three other girls sat at their own vanity tables. One girl tried to ignore the others, as if they were beneath her. The other two whispered together in their shared corner, alternately eyeing Clara and the silent girl. Clara wondered if they were plotting the start of World War III, their faces were so serious.

Clara had to bite her tongue to keep from laughing at that thought. To laugh outright would be rude, but it would also draw attention. That was part of her apprenticeship, too. Learning as much as she could without drawing too much attention.

A production assistant knocked on their door. "Clara, we need you on the set."

"No problem."

She got up, checking her makeup quickly before moving toward the door. The PA waited for her with a clipboard in hand. Clara had two weeks' worth of work on this feature film, so she got an honorary escort to and from the set. She smiled, straightening her leather miniskirt.

She was playing a friend of the best friend of the lead, so her scenes were numerous, though banal. They were all playing happy hookers, which Clara knew was a laugh. She never understood where Hollywood got their plots or why the public kept buying them. She shrugged one shoulder. That wasn't her concern. Whatever the public wanted was fine with her.

Her blonde hair was spiked out from her head like a crown of thorns. When she got to the set, the makeup and hair women descended on her, checking to see if she'd mussed anything while she waited. Of course, she hadn't. She was a professional.

She waited patiently while they gave her the once-over. Just to assert her authority, the head hairdresser applied more hair spray before letting Clara onto the set.

Clara smiled as she stepped under the hot lights. Only the noon sun in the desert was brighter. She felt at home immediately, and the tension ran out of her shoulders like water. The second lead nodded to her, giving her a surreptitious smile. Clara nodded back, careful not to look at the lead. The star of the production was a teenager who had worked in film and TV all her life. She had a starring role in a popular sitcom, and she was aware of her high status on the set. She hated Clara for no reason that she could understand. The girl felt inferior, which struck Clara as odd since she had never had more than two weeks' worth of work on any project, while this kid had cut her teeth on an Oscar.

Clara smiled to herself, careful to keep her eyes on the director and off the star. She should know by now not to speculate on other people's motives.

She listened as the director described what he wanted, speaking mostly to the star who stood brooding, her lower lip stuck out. The girl had been difficult all day, Clara gathered from the surface of the director's mind. She repressed a sigh. It looked like a simple scene was going to turn into a four-hour extravaganza.

Clara shrugged one shoulder. The more time it took, the more she learned. She caught the eye of the second lead and winked.

∽

They didn't finish filming until 8:30 that night. Clara knew the production had lost money while waiting for the lead to get ready to work, and she shook her head, bemused. It was a miracle any movie got made with the rampant incompetence and waste that went on.

Clara walked off the set, shrugging off the long day. She saw Pete waiting for her by the curb, and she slid into his Toyota.

"Hey, you." He smiled at her, and she leaned over and kissed him. "How'd it go?"

"Not bad," she said.

Clara never gossiped about what went on during production, though Pete often asked pointed questions. Once she was off the lot, she didn't want to talk about movies.

"Where are we heading?" she asked him.

"I thought we'd meet the guys over on Ventura, pick up a pizza, and just hang out."

"OK." Clara leaned back against the seat and relaxed.

Her shoulders ached. She would have to get him to give her a massage later.

They ate pizza in Pete's favorite restaurant, surrounded by his tech buddies, most of whom were grips and best boys. None of them were working at the moment, but they all had productions coming up, so they were relaxed and good-humored. Clara ate her pizza and sipped the tepid beer. She should have ordered soda. American beer was swill.

One best boy was gossiping about some big star who'd thrown a temper tantrum on the set. Clara didn't comment but watched him tell the tale. She glanced around the restaurant. Lucky for him, no one there was in the industry. She wondered why he was so careless to tell such gossip where he could be heard. Did he not know that talk like that could get him blackballed?

Clara watched as the others joined in with stories of their own, some about the same star, some about others. When Pete opened his mouth to tell one of his own, Clara laid her hand gently on his arm. She pitched her voice low, leaning over to whisper in his ear.

"Would you get me a coke, Pete?"

Pete's eyes widened behind his glasses. He could not remember the last time Clara had asked him for anything. He rose, his story forgotten. When he came back to the table, Clara had steered the conversation in the direction of union wages, which was a safer topic.

Pete joined in the fray enthusiastically, and they didn't leave the restaurant until midnight. They all left happy, a little drunk, and content that they'd single-handedly solved all the industry's problems. Clara took the car keys from Pete, and he knew her well enough by now not to protest.

"That was fun." He sighed, leaning back into the bucket seat.

Clara smiled. "It was. Just don't tell too many stories the way they did."

"Stories?"

"About stunts famous people pull on closed sets. There's a reason the sets are closed, Pete."

Pete frowned, sitting up straight. "But the stories are funny. Why shouldn't I tell them?"

Clara sighed. She knew she shouldn't get involved in his life this deeply, but she would feel guilty if she didn't at least warn him of the obvious. Guilt wasn't an emotion she'd a lot of experience with, but she genuinely liked him.

She watched him push his glasses further up his nose.

"All I'm saying, Pete, is that people talk. Wait until you want to retire, then write a tell-all book if you want. Just don't talk while you're still in the industry."

Pete laughed, his deep brown eyes sparkling. "Clara, you're being paranoid. We don't live in old school Communist Russia or something."

Clara shrugged one shoulder. "OK, Pete. Whatever you say."

She noticed that after that, whenever they were together in public, he didn't bad-mouth anyone. He saved all his stories until they were in bed. Clara was a good audience.

15

LOS ANGELES, 2015

CLARA ADJUSTED THE STRAPS OF HER RED SILK DRESS UNTIL THEY lay smooth against her shoulders. She turned to check her reflection in the full-length mirror. Her curves were lush under the smooth silk of the dress. She smiled at herself. She would have no trouble getting Willoughby's attention.

Robert Willoughby, Vice President of Development at Barnett Studios, was a married man who didn't fool around. He was the only married man Clara knew who didn't. That was part of the reason she'd chosen him to take her career up the next step of the ladder. He was a good man. And an honest one.

There was a knock at Clara's door, and she moved to open it. Pete stood there, holding a single red rose, smiling at her.

She grinned back at him. "Hi, Pete. Merry Christmas."

"It would be merry if you'd just say yes."

Clara laughed at him, the low, throaty laugh that within a year would be famous. She accepted the rose he offered and turned to the kitchen to put it in water.

Pete followed her into her studio apartment. She had furniture now, and he threw himself down on the daybed that also served as her couch. She didn't want to flaunt her money in front of the people she knew in the industry. She wanted to make her first million in films, then she could flaunt her inherited wealth. She wanted to look like she had earned it. If standing in front of a camera could be called earning it.

"Pete, we've been through this."

He was a first assistant director now, with more confidence than when she'd met him on the set of *Flaming Arrows*. He had stopped drinking, and he didn't sleep with as many women as before, hoping she would also stop sleeping with other men. She never did.

"I know we've been through it, Clara, but I want to go through it again."

His brown eyes stared back at her from behind his horn-rimmed glasses, and suddenly he reminded her of a math teacher she had lusted after at her girls' school years ago, before her mother had died. Clara smoothed his bangs back from his eyes and leaned down to kiss him.

"I'm not the marrying kind, Pete. I've told you that."

"Clara…" He breathed in the scent of her perfume, and as always, he found himself distracted from his train of thought.

Clara slid her hands down his shirt front and started to unfasten his jeans.

"Clara, we'll be late." His voice was hoarse, and his breath came fast.

"It's fashionable to be late in Hollywood. Haven't you heard?"

Her lips were on his, or he would have said that only the famous could be late to Robert Willoughby's parties. It was just as well. Clara wouldn't have listened.

They were three hours late to the party, and Clara was pleased with that. She didn't want to appear eager. Robert Willoughby hated the eager almost as much as he hated liars.

The man at the door didn't even check for their names on the list, but smiled at Clara, lost in her green eyes.

"Come right in, Miss —"

"Daniels." Clara smiled at him. "Clara Daniels."

She drew Pete with her into the house. He had worked in Hollywood for ten years, but he still had to stop himself from gaping around the rich and famous. His first assistant director's salary made him comfortable, and he worked steadily, but he would never know the opulence of Robert Willoughby's guest house, much less that of his mansion.

Clara scanned the crowd and found Mrs. Willoughby in the first few moments. People turned to stare at the girl in the red silk dress and the man she had in tow. A lot of women were dressed better, and many of the women were famous, but Clara had a presence that made even the most jaded give her a second glance.

She made her way gently through the crowd, smiling at those who smiled at her, and nodding to the few people she knew. Few day players had been invited to this party, and no extras of any kind. Clara had her SAG card, but she'd never had more than two weeks' worth of work on any project. That, however, was about to change.

Clara stopped in front of a short lady with deep brown hair. She was forty and her hair was dyed, but her smile was genuine as she turned to Clara.

"Hello. Have we met?"

"Not before tonight." Clara bestowed a rare gentle smile on Mrs. Willoughby.

This woman was as honest as her husband, and a good deal kinder. She had a lot to do with his current success, and Clara knew she would have a lot to do with the rest of his climb.

"Thank you for having us, Mrs. Willoughby. It's a pleasure to be invited to someone's home on Christmas Eve."

Mrs. Willoughby beamed at her, taking her hand. "I'm glad, honey. Are you new to Los Angeles?"

"No, ma'am. I've been here almost two years."

"Well, I'm glad to meet you."

Mrs. Willoughby nodded to Pete as she moved off, drawn away by the gentle hand of a friend who eyed Clara sardonically. Clara didn't give a damn what the friend thought. It was important to acknowledge her hostess, and she had done it. Mrs. Willoughby's friends and their suspicions were irrelevant.

Aunt April had bred Clara's manners into her bones. Clara would speak to her hostess again before she left. She had sacrificed a lot to become what she was becoming, but there were some standards that even she wasn't willing to part with.

Pete leaned close to Clara's ear and spoke softly. "I see Paul over there by the dessert table. I'm going to say hi."

"All right." Clara smoothed his bangs back on his forehead.

She was genuinely fond of him, and that constantly surprised her.

"I'll mingle," she said.

He pressed a kiss to her cheek and moved off, his hand sliding away from her waist reluctantly.

Clara took a glass of champagne off a passing tray, nodding to the servant who offered it. She sipped cautiously, scanning the room for Willoughby. She found him watching her, with a frown on his face.

He was forty-five and on his way to becoming head of the studio in another ten years or so. Clara smiled to herself, not dropping her gaze from his. With her help, he would finish his climb in less than two.

Willoughby's frown deepened, and he started to circle the room. Clara could read the surface of his thoughts and knew he was moving toward her. She didn't walk to meet him but stood still and let him come to her. By the time he reached her side, his frown was thunderous.

"So, you think you can make good with me by sucking up to my wife?"

Clara laughed at his rudeness. She smiled at him, enjoying someone for the first time in a long while. He hated manipulation, and he thought she was trying to use his wife to get to him.

"I always greet my hostess, Bob. I was raised to have manners. I'm not certain I can say the same about you."

She gestured to a nearby servant and took another champagne flute from his tray, relinquishing her empty one. The man had overheard her remark and stood wide-eyed, waiting to bolt at the first opportunity. He seemed to be one who lived in the house, not a rental for the evening, because he watched Willoughby's face as if waiting for an explosion that never came.

Willoughby reached over and took a glass of champagne for himself and drank, waving the man away. Clara didn't take her gaze off his face, watching as he decided what he thought of her. She knew it wouldn't take long.

"No one calls me Bob, by the way. The name's Robert." He glared at her, as if daring her to dispute him.

"If they call you that, they don't know you very well."

He stared at her for a long moment, his face blank. She listened to the wheels of his mind turning behind his eyes. The blue of his eyes seemed to catch fire, and he spoke low, with the tone of a threat.

"Who the hell are you?"

Clara smiled at him as if he'd introduced himself the way one would at a garden party.

She extended her hand. "I'm Clara Daniels. And you're Bob Willoughby, the man who's going to be the head of Barnett Studios in ten years."

He looked at her outstretched hand but didn't take it. He met her gaze, his anger gone.

"No one knows what the future holds."

"Not unless they build it."

Clara's hand didn't waver, and her gaze did not drop from his. The slow light of admiration crept into his eyes against his better judgment. She watched the first wall around his mind crumble as he extended his hand and slowly took hers. He didn't shake it but held it in his bearlike grasp as he looked at her.

"I'm faithful to my wife."

Clara laughed at the implication. "That's why I've chosen you."

He dropped her hand. "Chosen me? What the hell for?"

Clara's smile faded, and she took another sip from her champagne. "You're going to give me a role in your next picture."

She had made her play. Now it was up to him. She listened

intently to his thoughts, hoping she wouldn't have to start all over again with someone else.

Willoughby snorted and started to turn away. He stopped when the girl didn't move to follow him. He watched her out of narrowed eyes for a long moment before he spoke. For the life of him, he couldn't understand why he didn't just walk away. Something about the girl held him. Not her looks, though she had them, and not her cocky attitude. Cockiness was rampant in Hollywood. Both men and women had it, and it didn't make them any more attractive to him. It was something behind the girl's eyes, he realized. The hint of a mystery that he knew he would never solve. Robert Willoughby liked a challenge. He didn't walk away.

"Why the hell would I hire you?" he asked.

Clara gave him a gentle smile. She really did like this man. It was so refreshing to find someone in the industry that she genuinely liked.

"Because I'm going to make you rich."

"I'm already rich."

Clara set her empty glass on a nearby table. She scanned the room and saw Pete talking to a buddy he'd found by the dessert bar. He was eating chocolate mousse and gawking at the models nearby who, of course, ate nothing. Clara's smile widened at the sight of him. She didn't turn her attention back to Willoughby.

"You're going to be studio head within ten years. Would you agree?"

He shifted his weight but didn't answer until she looked at him.

"That's right."

Clara nodded. Another wall was beginning to crack between them.

"If you hire me, you'll be studio head in two."

Willoughby snorted, but she didn't drop his gaze. And after a moment, his sardonic smile faded.

"Two years is outrageous."

"Yes, but you're talented, and I'll sell. Give me a buddy role in your next film and then wait and see."

"I'm doing *Three Sisters and a Baby*. We start shooting next month. The buddy role has already been cast."

Clara shrugged one shoulder. She was completely relaxed as he scrutinized her, trying to search out her motives.

"It doesn't matter what movie you put me in. Just cast me in one that's shooting in the next six months, and I'll do the rest."

"Really?" He couldn't keep the sarcasm out of his voice. "That's all I need to do, and I'll be studio head?"

Clara met his gaze, not smiling. "Like I said, it'll take two years. But it will happen. I'll make it happen. And so will you."

It was a crucial moment. She listened avidly to every thought as it filtered through his mind. Willoughby looked into her eyes. She didn't disguise her ambition from him, but he didn't hear any cutthroat blood lust in her voice. She didn't want someone else's role. And she had a presence he'd rarely, if ever, seen. As he looked at her, he saw part of the secret that lay behind her eyes. She felt absolutely no fear.

"How old are you?" he asked.

"Eighteen." Clara smiled at him when he blinked.

He looked at her for another long, silent moment. Even years later, he never really knew why he answered her the way he had. But in that moment, he felt her certainty of success as a rock-solid fact, as if their success lay not in the future, but in the past.

"You're hired. I've got a role for you in *Standing in the Stream*. It's not a big one, but it's good."

Clara offered her hand. "That's great, Bob. You won't regret it."

He laughed a little under his breath. "I already do, kid." But he relaxed.

Clara offered him a canape that she took off a passing tray.

Willoughby took it and ate it, reflecting quietly for a moment.

"We've never met before," he said. "How did you manage to get an invitation to my party?"

Clara smiled the warm, slow smile that would make her famous. She met his gaze and didn't look away.

"Oh, I was never invited."

16

LOS ANGELES, 2019

THE BRIGHT SUN SHONE OFF THE PACIFIC, TURNING THE WATER A
deep blue. The smog had been washed away by heavy rains the
week before, and now the sky above Los Angeles gleamed as it
almost never did. Bob Willoughby's yacht was painted white, except
where the teak had been left bare, and the entire ship was lacquered
and gleaming.

Clara leaned back against the soft cushions of her deck chair,
and sighed. The sun soaked into her skin as the silence soaked into
her mind, broken only by the sound of the wind, the water lapping
against the keel of the boat, and the occasional stray thoughts from
Bob, which were easy to block out. Fred was there with them, but as
always, his mind was silent.

Clara was in such a state of clean well-being that she didn't
wonder why she'd never seen into Fred's mind. It was refreshing to
find a mind closed to her. Fred was one of the few people she no
longer wanted to manipulate.

Bob Willoughby waved to a deck hand, and he brought Clara a
tall glass of fruit juice mixed with vodka. She took the drink with a
smile. The deck hand blinked in the light of her eyes and moved
away quickly.

Clara sipped her drink, savoring the mixture of juice and alcohol on her tongue. As always on Bob's yacht, the drink was perfect. She couldn't remember the last time she'd been so relaxed.

"Bob, I've died and gone to Catalina Island."

Willoughby ran his fingers through his still-damp hair. He had just come up from a swim off the side of the yacht, ignoring Clara's laughing warning about sharks. He was dressed now in tennis whites, and only his hair was wet.

"Damn near, Clara. We're just half a mile out, I'd say."

She shaded her eyes against the sun as she looked at him. "You haven't thanked me for coming back to Barnett Studios yet, Bob."

Bob grunted and took a swig from his scotch. "If double your salary isn't thanks enough, I don't know what would be."

Clara laughed at his disgruntled tone. "I expected flowers at least, Bob."

He glowered. "What kind?"

She reflected a long moment, swirling her drink with the little umbrella attached to the side of the glass with a piece of lime.

"Hmmm… yellow roses with a tinge of pink at their tips. Roses just beginning to bloom."

Bob shook his head, smiling at her audacity. "Damn it, Clara, don't steal a project from me again. I almost lost my head over that damn *Desert Drift*."

Clara shrugged one shoulder, her eyes sparkling beneath the tinted lenses of her sunglasses, which she slid down from the top of her head.

"Well, Bob, I did warn you."

He leaned against the railing of his yacht, lifting his face to smell the salty air. "You did warn me, Clara. I just listened to Fred instead of you."

"And made an extra fifty million listening to me." Fred moved to sit by Clara's chair on the deck.

She smiled at him and took another sip from her glass. There was just enough vodka in the juice to make her mind pleasantly fuzzy without making her drunk.

In the sunny haze on the yacht's deck, Clara watched Fred

from behind her tinted lenses. He leaned back on his palms, letting the sun warm his face. As always, he was completely relaxed. The tanned muscles of his arms were visible under the sleeves of his golf shirt. Clara wondered if he ever actually played golf.

Fred felt her gaze and turned his head to smile at her. "So Bob's sending you flowers, Clara?"

She felt the same quiet elation as she always did when she was with him. The elation went to her head faster than the alcohol. She was used to drinking. She wasn't used to feeling giddy for no apparent reason. Today she didn't question it, but took her elation as her due, as part of the sun and the blue sky and the quiet peace of the ocean.

"Yellow roses, Fred," she replied. "With pink tips."

Willoughby snorted, rattling the ice in his scotch as he sat on the chair opposite Clara's.

"I don't know how you do it," he said.

She transferred her smile to the studio head, taking another sip of her drink.

"How I do what, Bob?"

"How you keep us all jumping."

Fred chuckled, and Clara laughed her throaty screen laugh. The deck hand who stood in attendance transferred his gaze to her face, and she laughed harder.

"You know damn well that you jump only when it suits you," Clara said.

She took off her sunglasses and handed her drink to the attendant. She leaned back against the soft cushions of her chair and closed her eyes. She felt the wind on her face and the sun on her hair. She couldn't remember ever feeling so at peace.

Bob gestured for another martini for Fred, but Fred held up his hand.

"No, thanks."

Willoughby watched the sunlight bring out the highlights in Clara's golden hair. Her pink silk dress swayed in the light breeze, her skirt covering her legs to her knees.

He shook his head ruefully. "Damn it, Clara. I should have slept with you when I had the chance."

She laughed at him, opening her eyes reluctantly to meet his gaze. "And ruin a beautiful partnership? Why the hell would you want to do that?"

Willoughby drank down the rest of his scotch and signaled for another. "As if you don't know."

He must be drunk, she mused, to make such idle comments.

"Bob, come off it. You've never cheated on Brenda, and you never will."

Willoughby met her gaze. For a long moment, he was caught in the green of her eyes. Then the deck hand brought his drink and he took it, grateful to have a reason to look away.

Clara turned her head and found Fred watching her, his gaze intent on her face. She raised an eyebrow but said nothing. Fred broke the silence, his voice hard, and he kept looking at Clara, and not at Bob. She felt for a moment as if he was trying to tell her something beneath his words, but she couldn't grasp it.

"Speaking of men Clara has slept with, what about that new kid you've got directing *Blast Away*, Bob? What's his name again? Charlie? Chuck?"

Willoughby nodded. "He's Clara's golden-haired boy."

Fred's smile didn't reach his eyes. She didn't understand what he was trying to say to her, but she could see that he was angry.

"He's one of your men, isn't he, Clara?" Fred asked.

She hated to be forced to talk business on what was supposed to be the last day of her vacation. She had to be on the set of *Blast Away* the next morning at 6:00 a.m., and she didn't want to think about movies. She turned her head lazily to look at Fred. She studied his face, but it revealed nothing. She wished she could hear the pattern of his thoughts so she could discern what game he was playing, if any. He simply watched her without blinking.

Clara decided to address the surface of Fred's question and leave the rest until he revealed his thoughts. She kept her voice light, though she could feel tension creeping into her neck and shoulders, in spite of the alcohol she had consumed.

"Chuck is a fabulous director who actually makes me look like I can act. When *Desert Drift* gets released nationwide, you're going to see some serious money being made."

"So I hear." Bob glowered at her.

She laughed at him, grateful to be able to take her eyes from Fred.

"What's this wunderkind's real name?" Fred asked.

"Charles Gratelli," Clara said. "I'm the only one who calls him Chuck."

"You would be."

Clara raised an eyebrow at his jibe. No one, not even he, spoke to her in that tone twice.

"Fred, if I didn't know better, I'd say you were jealous."

He held himself still, his face blank. He stood without another word and moved toward the ladder that led to the upper deck. Clara watched the play of his muscles under his shirt as he climbed the ladder and disappeared above their heads.

She met Willoughby's gaze. "What?"

His voice was as calm as if he were discussing a multi-million-dollar film deal. Bob was most serene when he felt the stakes were highest.

"You should put him out of his misery."

"How?" Clara quirked an eyebrow at him.

She forced a lightness into her voice that she didn't feel. She wouldn't discuss her personal affairs with anyone, not even Bob Willoughby.

"Should I shoot him? That wouldn't be sporting."

Bob shook his head and downed the rest of his drink. "Clara, I wonder sometimes if you have a heart."

"I've got a heart, Bob. It's safe in an offshore account."

In spite of her joking tone, Clara looked toward the ladder where Fred had disappeared. In that moment, sitting on the deck of that yacht in the summer sun, with the man she trusted most in the world, sadness threatened to dampen the clear light and ruin her day. Fred was different from all the others, but her feelings for him were irrelevant. Love wasn't a luxury she could afford to indulge in.

Clara kept her voice even and noticed that it took effort to do so. "Unfortunately, Bob, we don't live in Disneyland."

Willoughby looked at her, all trace of joking gone from his face. "No, Clara. But you hate Disneyland anyway."

She fell silent, closing her eyes. The sun was still warm on her face, but the festive atmosphere of the day was gone. She forced her mind away from Fred, away from the love she felt for him, away from problems that offered no opportunities and no solutions.

She wondered how long it would be before they could turn the yacht around and head back to Marina Del Rey. She had to call Donna about tomorrow's shoot.

When Clara walked into her house, the silence surrounded her like a cocoon. Margherita and the rest of the staff had left for the day, and the sun had set behind the bay.

Clara stepped into her living room, laying her bag down on a leather chair. That was when she saw the flowers on the marble table by the terrace door. A crystal vase filled with yellow roses with just a trace of pink at their tips. Roses that were just beginning to bloom. There was no card, so Clara knew they were from Fred.

17

LOS ANGELES, 2016

Clara smiled at the man guarding the door. He held a list on a clipboard, and her name wasn't on it. He waved her through anyway with a wink. He worked the door at every party Bob Willoughby threw, so he knew her by sight and let her pass. For once in her life, she didn't have to use her telepathic gift to manipulate someone into giving her what she wanted. She found that refreshing.

Clara scanned the crowd that wandered through the first floor of Stan Hendrickson's house. They milled around, watching each other like fellow sharks, all the time pretending they were far too casual to watch anyone or need anything. Clara smiled as she listened to their banter and compared it to the thoughts behind their eyes.

"I love that dress, Sylvia. Is it a Versace?" one woman asked, stopping just short of gushing on a new starlet who'd recently made her first feature film.

The woman's smile looked like a grimace to Clara. The woman knew that the young starlet was sleeping with her husband, which was how the starlet had gotten her role.

Clara moved through the crowd, shutting down her internal

radar. Her ability to read others' thoughts never went away, but she could focus her attention so that the sound of their minds was a low hum, like the white noise of the ocean. After so many years, Clara had gotten to the point where she didn't always listen to others' thoughts but was lulled a little by their low murmur. It was almost comforting.

Clara was nineteen but knew she passed for twenty-one. She watched with amusement as other women eyed her with hostility. They had no way of knowing she was no threat to them. None of them had what she wanted, and even if they had it, she was above stealing someone else's glory. Clara wanted glory of her own.

She took a glass of champagne off a passing tray and sipped it as she made her way out onto the terrace. There were candles floating in the heated pool, and she surveyed the crowd outside. Men stared at her, and she smiled. She didn't need to be a telepath to know what they were thinking.

Clara found that there was no one at the party who could do more for her than Bob Willoughby, so she decided to relax. She would just entertain herself tonight. Some of the most beautiful men in the world were wandering around that pool. She might as well sample one or two of them while she was there.

She sat on a lounge chair, and leaned back against it, sipping her drink. Her skirt rode up her thighs, showing a smooth expanse of tanned skin. She knew that tanning equaled cancer, but hosiery was inconvenient. Maybe she should switch to a garter belt, she mused, rather than risk her skin in the sun.

Clara was pondering this question, when a boy sat down beside her. His hair was dark, and his eyes were a deep cerulean blue. He could not have been more than five years older than she was, she guessed. She looked into his eyes and smiled. She could not read his thoughts. The champagne must have been beginning to cloud her vision.

Sometimes in a crowd, especially when she'd been drinking, an individual's thoughts would be swamped by the collective weight of all the other minds nearby. There had to be at least three hundred people in Stan's house that night. Clara dismissed her speculations with a shrug of one shoulder and watched the boy as he watched her.

"Hello." The boy's voice was deep and sent a shiver down her spine.

Clara felt almost young as she looked at him, watching the way his hand wrapped around his wine glass. A quiet sense of elation filled her and added flavor to her desire. She savored it. The taste of elation was new to her.

"Hello." She lowered her voice to match his.

He smiled at her but didn't seem ill at ease, a distinction that separated him from ninety-eight percent of the people at the party.

Clara let her eyes rove over his body. He was slender and wore faded jeans that hugged his narrow hips, and a t-shirt with the name of a film on it. She had never seen the film it mentioned but had heard that it was eminently forgettable. Clara wondered if he was an actor.

His gaze rested on her legs for a moment as he took another sip of his champagne. She knew the jade green of her dress matched her eyes, and that the silk flattered her figure where it clung.

The boy's eyes lingered on her hips and breasts before stopping at her face. In that moment, she changed her mind about him being an actor. He was too self-assured. It could have been bravado, of course, but Clara was fairly certain it wasn't. She wished for a moment that she could look into his thoughts, but then he spoke to her.

"You're the most beautiful woman here." His gaze never left her face.

Clara laughed her throaty laugh. "You have excellent taste."

The boy leaned forward for a moment, placing his empty glass on the concrete by his chair.

"I know it sounds like a standard pickup line, but I really mean it."

Clara smiled at him again, finishing her champagne. He took her glass and set it next to his own. She raised an eyebrow at his presumption but said nothing.

"Are you an actress?" His gaze began to stray down her body again.

She laughed, and the sound brought his gaze back to her face.

"Not yet," she replied, "but I will be."

He watched her for a long moment, as if he could see past her eyes.

"You know, I think you will."

Clara rose, letting the silk of her skirt slide down her legs. She stretched, giving him an unobstructed view of her body. He stood, and she felt her breath catch at his nearness. He wore light cologne that carried a faint trace of sandalwood.

She extended her hand to him, and he took it. She moved to lead him away from the crowd but found him leading her. Clara found that she enjoyed the novelty of being led. She did so much leading herself, sexually and otherwise, and she realized that she was tired of it.

She followed him up the large staircase. She thought he was taking her to a bedroom on the second floor and was surprised when he led her higher. On the third floor, there were a few unoccupied bedrooms, but he didn't lead her into any of those. He drew her into a bathroom the size of a closet and closed the door.

Clara laughed, and the sound reverberated off the oak paneled walls.

"This is novel, I must say."

He smiled at her, brushing his fingers against her cheek before sliding his hand up into her hair.

"It's private. Most of the bedrooms in this house aren't."

"Hidden cameras?" Clara joked, enjoying the feel of her pulse quickening as he touched her.

"You could say that."

His lips trailed from her cheekbone to her throat, and she leaned against him.

"I wouldn't want to wind up on YouTube," she said.

She felt his laugh against her skin, and she shivered.

"No," he said, "we wouldn't want that."

He was silent then, running his fingers over her thighs as he drew her skirt up to her waist. He pushed her back against the door. It was a sturdy door made of oak, and the lock was sound, so he leaned their combined weight against it.

They made love quickly, moving together as if they were made for it. They lost their breath together, and when it was over, they stared into each other's eyes. Clara had the odd sense that she would find it hard to look away.

"I've never done this before," he said.

She laughed. "You'd never know it."

He smiled at that, kissing her. "I mean, I've never done this in a bathroom."

"That makes two of us. Walk me to my car?"

He kissed her temple, and she thought for a moment he might say something more. Then the moment was gone, and he simply took her hand.

He walked downstairs with her. People smirked to see them leave together, thinking he had made a conquest. Clara figured she had done the conquering, but she'd known all her life that what people thought about her rarely resembled the truth.

The boy walked with her to her tiny Japanese car. He took the key from her, unlocked the door and held it for her. Clara was strangely touched by the gesture, and hesitated before she got in.

"I suppose exchanging numbers would be a bad idea," he said.

She looked at him for a long moment, shocked that she was actually tempted to do just that. Her good sense overrode her strange mood.

"Probably."

He leaned down and kissed her softly, then stepped back and let her go.

"See you." She slipped into her car.

He closed the door behind her. "I hope so."

She smiled at him as she started the engine. He stepped back and gave her a jaunty wave. Not until she was on the freeway headed back to her apartment in the Hollywood Hills, did she realize that she hadn't asked his name.

18

LOS ANGELES, 2016

CLARA PICKED UP THE PHONE AND TURNED OFF HER VACUUM. SHE was having a day of spring cleaning, though it was the middle of July. Her golden hair was tied back in a kerchief, and she pulled the cloth away from her ear as she picked up her cell.

"Hello."

"Clara, you're in."

Clara smiled at the sound of Bob Willoughby's voice. They'd been working together for almost a year, and she still found him charming.

"I'm in what, Bob?"

"The new Cleopatra movie."

"That's fabulous."

Clara swiped her dust cloth over the mahogany end table. She had only a little furniture in her apartment, but they were all good pieces.

"Am I her maid or something?"

There was a long silence on the other end of the line. When Bob spoke, she could hear the excitement in his voice.

"No, Clara. You're playing Cleo."

Clara stopped moving her hand over the table and held very still.

"What?"

"You're Cleopatra, kiddo. I just got the green light from Frank."

Bob referred to the current head of Barnett Studios without the usual shade of contempt in his voice. That's how Clara knew he was serious.

"Holy shit."

She was silent for a moment, and he laughed.

"I never thought I'd see the day when you were struck speechless."

Clara sat on the hardwood floor of her great room. The afternoon sun slanted in from her wall of windows. As she looked outside, she saw a bird flying high over the hills.

"Bob, I've got a problem."

"What?"

"I'm blonde."

Bob laughed so hard she heard him lay the phone down on his desk. She smiled, listening to him. He rarely laughed out of genuine amusement.

"Jesus, Clara, you never stop surprising me."

"That's why you keep me around." Clara stretched like a cat in the sunlight, pulling off the kerchief and letting her hair fall free over her shoulders.

"It's not official yet, so don't go around telling people."

It was Clara's turn to laugh. "Bullshit, Bob. You wouldn't have called me if they hadn't already made up their minds."

In her mind's eye, she could see him grinning, and she heard that grin in his voice.

"Yeah, it's set. The director just doesn't know it yet."

"Do they need me to come in and talk to him?"

"Nah, I wouldn't set you lose on the poor bastard. He's not reluctant, just unaware."

Clara smiled, leaning back on her hands, watching the muscles of her legs as she stretched.

"We need to celebrate," she said.

"I agree."

"Get Brenda and meet me at West. I feel like eating steak."

"When?"

"How's seven sound?"

"Great."

She listened to his chair squeak as he leaned back in it. She knew he was looking out his window over the studio lot.

"Bob, this is going to make you studio head."

"Now, Clara, it'll take one more project and you know it."

"Wait and see. Two months after this one opens, you'll be sitting in the big chair."

Bob snorted. "Well, Clara, I do know that it'll make you famous."

"I won't wear a wig."

He laughed at her joke, and Clara smiled.

"Hell, no. We'll get you the best dye-job in town. Now let me call my wife."

"You haven't told her yet?"

"Before telling you? What kind of fool do you think I am?"

Clara smiled. "See you tonight."

"The studio's buying, am I right?" Willoughby asked.

Clara grinned, feeling lighter than she had when she picked up the phone.

"You're damn right they are."

She heard him laughing as she hung up.

Clara smiled at Willoughby as he raised his glass to her.

"To the next Katherine Hepburn."

Clara laughed, taking a sip of her wine. "Who the hell will that be, Bob?"

"You, and you know it."

She grinned at him, winking at Brenda beside him. "Don't you think I need to learn to act first?"

"You act well enough." He started cutting into his steak.

Brenda leaned over and touched Clara's hand.

"Your smile will sell, Clara. And your eyes."

She smiled at Bob's wife, squeezing her hand. Brenda was the loveliest woman Clara could remember meeting. She didn't belong in Hollywood, and Bob wouldn't have survived there without her.

"Thank you, Brenda. You'll have to come watch me on the set and bolster my spirits. I'll be feeling my lack of ability with Pat Mulligan standing in front of me. Bob, how the hell did they pick an Irishman to play Caesar, anyway?"

Bob shrugged one shoulder, pouring himself more wine. "I don't know. He's a great actor. Women and men love him. Are those reasons enough for you?"

Clara grinned at him, spearing a piece of filet with her fork. "Now, I haven't seen the script yet, so let me get this straight. The movie ends before Cleo is twenty-three?"

Willoughby nodded. "We've cut it in half, and we've made the writer fill out the first two acts. It was like a damn history lesson before, and God knows no one is going to pay to see that."

"So they cut out Marc Antony?" Clara kept her voice mild.

"Marc who?" Bob met her gaze, and she saw fire in his eyes. "Who, I ask you, gives a damn about Marc Antony? He lost."

Clara laughed and reached for her wine. People in the restaurant heard her throaty laugh and turned to look at her. Some knew Bob Willoughby, but no one knew who she was. Yet.

"Yeah, we had to deal with the writer on that one," Bob said. "Turns out, he's the nephew of one of the producers, so we actually had a fight on our hands for about five minutes." He snorted. "I cleared that crap up. No one wants to see a docudrama about some loser."

Clara suppressed her smile. "So, when do we start filming?"

"Next week. You'll need to go in and get your hair dyed tomorrow. They want to test you again with the dark hair." Bob scrawled a name and an address on the back of his business card. "See this guy. He's the best."

"I had no idea you knew so much about women's hair, Bob." Clara's eyes sparkled as he glared at her.

Brenda laid her hand over her husband's and laughed. "Clara, you're a breath of fresh air. No one teases Bob but you."

Clara winked at her, and Bob grunted.

"Damn right," he said.

Brenda smiled serenely. "It's good for him."

Clara raised her glass. "To Bob Willoughby. The next head of Barnett Studios."

Brenda lifted her glass. "Here, here."

Bob didn't smile but drank, his gaze never leaving Clara's face.

19

LOS ANGELES, 2016

BOB WILLOUGHBY'S VOICE WAS CALM OVER THE PHONE. CLARA stood on her deck, running her fingers through her hair and gritting her teeth. Bob never asked favors of her, but he was asking for one now.

"Clara, it won't kill you to spend a weekend at this spa."

She took a deep breath, trying to hold onto her temper. "I know it won't kill me, but spas make me nervous. They make you eat rabbit food and run four miles a day. No thanks."

She could hear the smile in Bob's voice. "It's not that kind of place. They serve filet mignons and the best wines. They pamper you and massage you and indulge your every whim."

Clara raised an eyebrow. "Really? Every whim?"

Willoughby heard the suggestive tone in her voice but ignored it. "Clara, it's a great two days. You see some pretty country, you drink some wine, you shack up with a masseur or two, and the studio pays for it all. What's not to like?"

"Bob, why does this Donna woman have to come? I don't deal well with women."

Clara knew she sounded petulant, but she was closing on the

purchase of her first house on Monday, and her lawyer was making her frantic.

"Brenda loves you."

"Brenda's different, Bob, and you know it."

"Trust me on this one, kid. You do not want to start a three-month shoot with a woman you hardly know. Donna is a fine manager, the best in the business, and she's serious about getting to know her clients. She wants to spend a little time with you to learn your quirks."

"So she can accommodate them, right?"

"That's the idea."

Clara sighed. She could use a weekend out of the city.

"Where is this spa again?"

She could hear Bob's grin in his voice. "Donna has directions. She'll pick you up."

"Are you kidding?"

"She doesn't want you inconvenienced."

Clara snorted.

"Get used to it, kid. This is the way it'll be once you're famous."

"I'll have Donna at my beck and call?"

"Among other people."

Clara laughed. "All right, Bob. We'll see what we see."

Donna was a thin woman in a sophisticated black suit and tasteful gold jewelry. Her hair was black and cut into a pageboy. She drove a sporty red Maserati, which made Clara wonder who she'd represented in the past.

Donna got out of the car and extended her hand. Clara shook it.

"Hi, Clara. Let me take that."

Donna hoisted Clara's duffle bag into the car and opened the passenger door for her.

"Sorry we're a little informal." Donna gunned the engine of the expensive car. "I would have gotten a limo, but Bob said you were interested in a casual weekend."

Clara delved into the other woman's mind, suspecting her of being flippant. Donna wasn't kidding, however. She had a completely serious mind and felt that every moment with her client held great import. She represented only one actor at a time, something practically unheard of in Hollywood. She backed each client with a blind obsession that was legendary. Bob said she would cost more than any other manager they could get, but that she was worth every cent. Clara had taken his word for it, since she didn't see the need for a manager in the first place.

Sitting in the car, watching Donna maneuver deftly through afternoon traffic, Clara began to re-assess. Donna had almost as strong a will as she did, and with none of her advantages. She liked the woman already.

"I've reserved an ocean-front suite for you. I didn't want you to be disturbed this weekend. You start shooting *Queen of Egypt* in a week, and you need your head clear." Donna spoke rapidly, pulling onto Highway 1, cutting off an eighteen-wheeler.

Clara smiled as Donna took a hairpin turn at fifty miles an hour. She sat back, the sun warm on her face, and enjoyed the way the wind felt in her hair.

For some reason, Donna wanted to look after her this weekend. And by some miracle, she was competent enough to do it. Clara had never been taken care of in her life, but two days of it couldn't hurt.

She watched a seagull wheel overhead and took in the sunlight glinting on the surface of the ocean beside them. She sighed, leaning back against the leather seat, and prepared herself to be pampered.

Clara had heard of star treatment, of course, but she'd never paid any attention to it, since it was never directed at her. At the spa on the coast of Monterey, she got her first taste of it.

Donna had called ahead and had told the staff that Clara was an up-and-coming starlet with money to spend. She had added that Clara was someone who might have a good deal of influence in the future, and that it was a good idea to court her business. So, when Donna drove the Maserati under the awning of the spa's main building, three men stepped outside to meet them. One pulled the luggage out of the trunk while another opened Clara's door. The third man, the manager on-duty, bowed to her and kissed her hand.

Clara almost laughed but stopped herself. This man was serious about his business. Even if she thought his business a foolish one, she respected his intent. She smiled at him and held still until he released her hand.

Donna stepped forward. "We'd like to see Miss Daniels' suite. She needs to get settled in." Her voice was brisk and polite.

The manager bowed to her. "Of course. Come this way, madam. Miss Daniels."

Clara followed, bemused. They made a small parade through the lobby as the manager led them across the plush carpet and past the built-in waterfall. The other two men trailed in their wake, baggage in hand. Clara felt music should be playing to add the final touch to their march. As she was thinking it, a woman sat at the piano in the lobby and began to play Tchaikovsky. Clara bit her tongue hard, and the pain kept her from laughing out loud.

Her suite was beautifully decorated in pale greens and beige. One wall was made of glass, and a sliding door opened onto the beach. Clara could hear the crash of the waves. Next to the heat of the desert, she loved the sound of ocean.

She wandered through the suite as Donna spoke with the manager, giving directions for the meal that night and ordering a massage for Clara before dinner.

The bedroom also looked out onto the sea and was decorated in the same soft greens. Clara felt soothed already, and she hadn't realized she needed soothing.

One of the staff brought her bag into the room and bowed to her before setting it down. She smiled at him and winked. He didn't even blink but let her precede him into the den.

"It's gorgeous, Donna. I'm impressed."

"We're glad you're pleased," the manager said, bowing yet again.

The other two servants bowed as well and went to stand by the door. Donna pulled cash from her Armani bag and dispensed it liberally, including the manager in the windfall.

"If you need anything, please call me," the manager said.

Donna nodded and closed the door behind him. Clara waited until she heard their thoughts disappear down the hall. Then she laughed, sprawling on the plush sofa that faced the windows.

"Damn, Donna, I've never seen anything like that, even when I was a kid."

"It does have its own theatrical flair, doesn't it?" She turned to the bar in the corner. "Do you need a drink?"

"No, thanks." Clara stretched luxuriously. "I think I'll have a nap."

"Your masseur will be here in an hour. Would you like me to call and wake you before he gets here?"

"Don't bother. I'll have to get naked for him anyway."

She watched as Donna caught the underlying meaning of the statement, and saw a gleam come into Donna's blue eyes. Clara simply smiled and felt her manager's amusement from across the room. Donna met Clara's gaze evenly, without a hint of judgement. They understood each other. Clara couldn't remember ever feeling that way about another woman, even for a moment.

Her manager moved toward the door. "I'm in room twenty if you need anything."

"Do you have an ocean view?"

Donna turned back to face her, smiling, her hand on the doorknob.

"Of course."

Later that night, Clara sat with Donna on the terrace outside her suite. They had finished the duck l'orange and were working on their second bottle of wine. Clara leaned back into the soft cushions of her chair and sighed. She had done some calisthenics with her masseur after her massage and had made an appointment to see him again the next day. She felt completely relaxed as she always did after sex, her joints fluid and pliant. She lit a cigarette and watched as the smoke trailed heavenward.

Donna poured more wine into both glasses, then kicked her shoes off and propped her feet on the railing. The stars were bright above their heads. They were miles from the nearest city, so there was no pollution to block the stars.

Clara was amazed that Donna had sat with her in silence for almost an hour. She'd never known a woman who could endure silence, with the exception of her Aunt April.

She looked into Donna's mind and found that the woman wasn't planning the next day's adventures, but was simply listening to the ocean, letting her thoughts drift. With all her frenetic energy, Clara hadn't realized that Donna was also capable of being at peace.

"So, did you sleep with him?" Donna took a sip of her wine.

Clara released a long line of smoke. "Of course."

"I don't mean to pry. I was just curious." Donna was silent for a long moment. "I never do anything like that."

"Have sex?"

Donna looked over and laughed. Clara was surprised that her laugh was soft, almost girlish.

"I have sex. Not often enough. No, I mean having sex with a man just because I find him attractive, even if I just met him five minutes before."

Clara shrugged one shoulder, stubbing out her cigarette in the crystal ashtray on the table.

"Once you do it the first time, it's easy after that. You just have to decide to take that leap, and then jump. I never even think about it anymore."

"Who was your first random encounter?" Donna asked.

Clara laughed. "Jesus, Donna. You make it sound like space aliens or something."

Donna laughed, too. "No, I mean, who was your first random partner?"

Clara hesitated for half a second. "My stepfather."

She watched Donna as she said that, wondering what her reaction would be. She didn't feel a wave of judgment from her. Donna simply thought about what she had said, not offering any emotion in connection with it. Her estimation of her manager rose higher.

"He doesn't sound all that random, if he was your stepfather," Donna said at last.

"You've never met him. Trust me. Darren was as random as they come. You'll have to take my word for it."

They sat in silence, listening to the ocean as it crashed onto the shore in the darkness. Clara never knew why she had been so open with Donna that night. She was never so open with her again, though they worked together for years after that. Clara wondered if the moon had been full, or if the ocean had lulled her into a sense of complacency.

When she met Donna for breakfast the next morning, the sense of intimacy between them had slipped away with the outgoing tide. They talked shop, outlining their strategy for dealing with the myriad producers of *Queen of Egypt*.

Clara never knew if Donna started having random flings. She never asked.

20

STUDIO CITY, 2016

It was Clara's first day on the set of *Queen of Egypt*. She looked around the trailer, even delved into the refrigerator. The little bottles of Evian that Donna had insisted on were lined up like sentinels. Clara closed the refrigerator and sat on the overstuffed sofa with a sigh. The trailer wasn't home, but it wasn't bad. It was definitely a step up from any trailer she'd been assigned before on a movie set.

A young woman burst into the trailer without knocking. "Hi, Miss Daniels. Oh!"

The girl stood frozen in place, a look of horror on her face. Clara glanced around, expecting to see a lizard on the floor or something. There was nothing there.

Clara smiled at the girl. "What wrong?"

"Oh, Miss Daniels, I'm so sorry. I should have knocked. I—"

Clara laughed. The girl jumped at the sound as if Clara had shot at her.

"Calm down. What's the problem?"

"I just came into your trailer without knocking." The girl was so pale that Clara was starting to worry about her.

"I think we can let it pass this once. Who are you?"

"Oh." The girl straightened her back, a little color coming into her face. "I'm your assistant, Lila."

Clara smiled and stood up, extending her hand. "Hi, Lila. I'm Clara. Nice to meet you."

The girl's smile was like a sunrise across her face. "You're so nice! I thought…" She blushed.

Clara laughed. "You heard I was a bitch, right?"

The girl turned even redder.

Clara swallowed her laughter. "Well, I am. To the producers. But not to the hired help. Come in and have a soda."

The girl looked confused but came out of the doorway where she'd been lingering. She sat gingerly on the chair Clara offered her, as if it were packed with explosives and set to go off under her. She fidgeted while Clara opened a can of soda and handed it to her.

The girl looked at her, her mouth opening and closing like a fish. "Miss Daniels…"

"You need ice with this? I'll bet there's baccarat crystal in here somewhere." Clara started opening cabinets.

The girl leaped to her feet. "Miss Daniels! You're not supposed to wait on me. I'm supposed to—"

"I know, I know. Assist me. And believe me, you will. But it's your first day. Kick back a minute and have a drink." Clara sat on the plush sofa, her own soda in hand.

The girl sat primly on the edge of her overstuffed chair. She looked uncomfortable. Clara leaned back and sighed. She wondered when the makeup people would come and fetch her.

"Miss Daniels?"

"Yes, Lila?"

"Maybe we should talk about, um, you know, what you expect from me."

"Well, right now I expect you to drink that soda."

The girl dutifully took a sip, then tried again. "About my job, Miss Daniels. Is there anything you would like me to do? Bring you a certain newspaper, get you novels…"

"Bring me cocaine?"

The girl's eyes went wide.

"I'm kidding. I don't do hard drugs."

Clara finished her soda and checked her watch. She was due in makeup in about ten minutes.

"Your job is to answer my phone and to keep everyone but the producers and the director off my back. You run interference for me, and I bring you sodas. Deal?"

Lila sat looking at her in silence for a long moment. She blinked. Then she started to laugh.

Clara smiled. "We'll get along just fine."

Clara was dressed for her first scene. She stood on the set, looking at the pseudo-Egyptian trappings. She wondered if they were going to add a live cat to the set in their effort to achieve authenticity. She knew then that her mind was wandering, and she forced herself to focus.

She watched the grips set up the lighting and felt a butterfly swoop into her stomach. She almost laughed. She never got nervous. It wasn't as if she were a real actor or something.

She looked across the set and saw Pat Mulligan standing there, as large as life and twice as gorgeous. The butterfly in her stomach did an aerial dive. Clara wondered for the first time in her life if she'd bitten off more than she could chew.

She turned to face him fully and saw him smiling at her. The butterfly disappeared. Of course, she knew what she was doing.

Clara strode over to him and extended her hand. "Mr. Mulligan. It's a pleasure to meet you."

His smile warmed, and he took her hand in his, holding it without shaking it.

"The pleasure is mine, Miss Daniels. And please, call me Pat."

His deep accented voice ran up her spine like warm fingers, and she shivered. Clara took a deep breath in an effort to keep her lust under control. It almost worked.

"Well, you'll have to call me Clara, then."

He smiled, still holding her hand. "Of course."

Later that night, Clara watched the last of the twelve producers leave her trailer. Donna stood by the door, her hand on the lock, waiting to see if another knock came. One didn't. Donna threw the bolt, and Clara leaned back on her sofa, sighing.

Clara was wearing jeans and a t-shirt, her face clean of makeup. She had sent Lila home when the fifth producer had knocked. Donna stood against the door, though it was already locked, smoking a cigarette. Clara groaned.

"Do you think those asshats really liked my work, or were they just bullshitting?"

Clara hadn't opened up to look into their minds. She didn't feel like swimming in cesspools this late in the evening.

Donna shot her a look, taking another drag off her cigarette. "Do you care?"

Clara laughed for the first time since she'd come off the set. "Hell, no."

"I didn't think so."

Donna poured Clara a drink from the bar and handed it to her without a word.

"I ache all over," Clara said.

"Being a star is a lot of work."

Clara laughed. "Shit, I wish somebody had told me that."

Donna smiled and lit another cigarette.

21

NEW YORK, 2016

Clara sat in the plush leather chair at the head of the table. Movie reviewers from all over the country sat around her, fiddling with their pens and their cell phone recording apps. They were there for the studio-sponsored press junket to discuss *Queen of Egypt*. Donna stood at Clara's elbow, as protective as a mother hawk, ready to swoop down and whisk her away at the first sign of trouble. Clara smiled. She didn't expect any trouble.

One of the studio's gophers brought her a fresh soda. Clara accepted it with a nod and poured it over ice. She waited for one of the members of the press to speak.

"So, Miss Daniels, how long have you been an actress?"

Clara smiled, sipping her soda to buy a moment of time. She repressed the urge to tell the truth, that she couldn't act her way out of a paper bag. She had to remember that she wasn't really talking to the people around this table, but to the public who would read their words.

Clara kept her voice low and thoughtful, looking off into space for a moment as if pondering the question.

"Well, I suppose I've always wanted to act, ever since I was a little girl. My first real job was as Rose in *Standing in the Stream*."

"I saw that," one woman gushed, pushing her glasses up onto the bridge of her nose. "You were brilliant."

Clara almost asked the woman if they were talking about the same film but looked into the woman's mind. In spite of her profession, she was a true fan and had seen every movie Clara had ever made, even *Flaming Arrows*. Clara softened. It was a valuable lesson to learn, that some press were actually public in disguise.

She smiled at the woman, focusing her charm on her as if she were the only other person in the room.

"Thank you. I was pretty green on that film, but the director was good, so it all worked out."

Clara let the lie slip from her tongue easily before raising her glass to her lips again. The woman wrote the quote with dogged determination, as if the Pope himself had spoken Holy Writ, and Clara began to feel the first thrill of power.

Another reviewer spoke up, a man who wrote for *Toronto Today*. He smiled at Clara as if he were Don Juan.

"How did you enjoy working with Pat Mulligan, Miss Daniels?"

Clara turned her focus on him and grew serious. "It was an honor."

Another woman spoke, jumping in before the man could ask a follow-up question.

"Were you at all intimidated by Mr. Mulligan?"

"No." The truth slipped from Clara's tongue before she took a moment to think. She breathed deeply and smiled a charming smile. "Mr. Mulligan was the soul of graciousness. He was always a gentleman, and it was a pleasure to work with him."

"Miss Daniels." The reviewer from the *Minneapolis Herald* raised one hand. "How did you feel playing the Pharaoh Cleopatra?"

Clara smiled. "Now that was intimidating."

There was soft laughter around the table, and Clara could feel Donna begin to relax a little. Donna leaned over and lit a cigarette, never taking her eyes off the press. One of the lackeys running the press junket came in and gestured at her watch. Donna nodded to her, taking a drag off her cigarette. There was time for only one more question.

"What's your next project, Miss Daniels?"

"Nothing is set in stone. But let's say that I hope to take a trip to the Amazon River Delta before I see you all again."

There was a blockbuster in the works about a team of zoologists who were chasing a giant snake down the Amazon river. The female lead hadn't been cast yet. Clara decided to make a bid for it publicly, to back up Willoughby's maneuvering to get her the role.

"I'm afraid that's all the time Miss Daniels has, folks," Donna said. "Thank you very much. I believe Pat Mulligan is up next. For those of you who haven't met him, you're in for a treat." She took Clara's elbow and ushered her out without missing a step.

Clara laughed under her breath. "Damn, Donna. I didn't know you could be so decisive. How manly."

Her manager shot her a look, running her manicured hand through her dark hair.

"I didn't want them to keep you any longer. We need to make our flight."

Clara opened her mouth to make another lame joke but held off when she saw Pat Mulligan coming down the hallway. He was a huge man in person, even more physically alluring than he was on screen. He smiled at her and stopped. His entourage formed around him, trying to draw him into the press room. He didn't say a word but gave them a look that sent them all back a few steps. As if by magic, a space cleared around them. He was throwing off the studio's time schedule. But he was Pat Mulligan. The studio would wait.

"Hello, Clara."

She felt a shiver run up her spine, as it always did whenever he spoke her name. She smiled at him, admiring the glint of his hazel eyes. He was a fine specimen of a man. She wondered, and not for the first time, if he had the gift.

"Hello, Pat."

Donna looked away, taking a step down the hall and drawing her cell phone out of her bag. She turned her back discreetly to them, and Clara smiled. Donna thought they were sleeping together.

Clara looked at him and almost sighed. Didn't she wish.

"How was it?" he asked, his brogue lightly flavoring the question.

Clara smiled at him, shrugging one shoulder. "It seemed to go well. I've never done one of these before."

He smiled, pitching his voice low. "I'm sure you did well."

"Good luck yourself."

He laughed, as she knew he would, as he started to move down the hallway and away from her.

"I've never needed luck." He winked at her, and her smile broadened.

Someday she might actually ask him whether or not he could see into people's souls. It wouldn't surprise her at all if he could.

Clara sighed as the door shut behind him.

"You've got it bad, huh?" Donna asked as they started walking to the car waiting for them outside.

"Lust?" Clara said. "Yes."

"Oh," Donna murmured, "I thought…"

Clara laughed, the dreaminess gone from her eyes. "You thought I was in love with him?"

Donna shifted uncomfortably, and Clara laughed harder. She caught her breath as they walked out into the rain. It seemed that New York was always gray when Clara was there.

"Oh, Donna, you've got a lot to learn about me."

22

LOS ANGELES, 2019

"That's a wrap. Cut and print."

Clara smiled as the crew around her broke into applause. The space thriller *Blast Away* was in the can. Someone shouted a little. One grip pulled out a bottle of champagne and started filling glasses.

"Don't get that on the cables for God's sake," the head electrician griped.

Clara laughed when she heard that. Chuck came over and put one arm around her shoulders, carefully, as if she were made of very thin glass.

"Thank you, Clara." His voice was soft, and she had trouble hearing him over the noise of the crew as they started to strike their equipment.

"For what, Chuck?"

He smiled at the use of his nickname. "Nobody else calls me that, you know."

"After this picture hits the box office, they'll all be calling you Mr. Gratelli, and nothing else."

Charles smiled his shy smile, his blond bangs falling into his eyes. "I really do want to thank you."

"Chuck, you're the one who does all the work. I just stand here and look good."

He frowned a little. "That's not true. And that's not what I mean." He looked directly into her eyes, and she found that she couldn't look away. "Thank you for this chance. They would never have hired me for this film if you hadn't forced them to."

Clara almost laughed. She started to shrug his arm off her shoulders and dismiss him with a quick kiss on the cheek but stopped mid-motion, caught by the light in his clear blue eyes. He seemed so young to her, almost innocent. Clara took a chance, opened her mind and read his thoughts. She quickly discovered that he was neither as young nor as innocent as she had assumed.

She decided to pay him the compliment of respecting him. "You're welcome, Charles. It was my pleasure."

"I know everybody thinks you're a hard woman—"

Clara laughed. "A hard-ass, you mean."

"Well… yes. But I have found you a delight to work with."

She didn't speak for a long moment. Clara was touched by the compliment, and she hadn't been moved by praise in years.

She cleared her throat. "Thank you, Charles. You make me look good, you know. People watching our last two films will actually think I have talent."

He looked into her eyes. "You do, Clara. Don't let anyone tell you otherwise."

She listened to his thoughts. He was telling her the truth as he saw it.

"Thank you."

"And keep calling me Chuck." His smile was a slow light across his face. "I like it."

Clara kissed his cheek. "I will." She pulled away from him. "Don't forget about me once the studios start courting you. I may need you to hire me again sometime."

She made the comment as a feeble joke to break the tension, but Charles was serious.

"You can count on it, Clara."

"Well, I've got to catch my flight."

"Sure. I'll see you when you get back."

He raised a hand, and she waved back, moving out of the circle of cameras and equipment. A lot of it was already down and being stowed away. Clara made her way to her dressing room at the far side of the studio building, where she found Fred waiting for her outside the door. She smiled at him, but he didn't smile back.

"That was a touching scene."

"What?" Clara blinked at the hostility in his tone.

She thought she would laugh at him and shrug him off but surprised herself by not dismissing him. Instead of walking past him into her dressing room, she faced him and waited. Her assistant passed them and slipped inside discreetly.

Fred stared at her. "So, is he your next victim?"

"I don't have victims, Fred."

She wasn't sure, but she thought she heard pain in his voice.

"You know what I'm saying. Are you taking him to bed?"

"Who?"

"You know damn well who."

Clara looked into his eyes. She hadn't been spoken to in that tone in over six years. She waited for anger to rise and grab her by the throat until she unleashed it on the man standing in front of her. To her surprise, no anger came. She simply stood looking at the pain in his eyes. She couldn't read his thoughts, but his face was an open book.

"No. Chuck and I aren't lovers."

Fred's expression didn't change, but she saw a little of the tension drain out of his shoulders.

"So, when are you going to bed with him?"

"I'm not."

Instead of being amused by his jealousy and mocking him with it, Clara felt flattered. And pleased.

She stepped into her dressing room, and he followed her. Her dresser stepped forward and helped her out of her leather space suit. Clara reached for a soft silk robe, and Lila helped her into it.

"Lila, could you bring Mr. Walker and me some champagne? I think they have some on the set."

"Sure, Miss Daniels."

Lila raised an appreciative eyebrow in Fred's direction, but he didn't even glance at her. She smiled as she left with the wardrobe woman, closing the door behind them.

Clara stood looking at Fred. His eyes were a deeper blue because he was angry. She moved to him and kissed his jaw, wrapping her arms around his waist. It was the first time she had touched him since the night they'd slept together at her house, months before.

"Are you angry with me?" she asked.

"I don't know." He didn't yield to her embrace.

Clara trailed her lips over his throat, and she felt him give way just a little.

"You seem angry."

She pressed herself against him, and felt his arms come around her. He held her but didn't try to pull her any closer. There was a long silence. Clara could think of nothing glib to say. She could only think of the pain she'd seen in his face, and that she loved him.

As she found herself looking into the blue of his eyes, she realized that she could go all her life without ever finding someone who loved her as he did. That truth was startling, but it was there, silent, waiting for her, as if it had been waiting only for her to turn her own mind off and see it.

The silence stretched between them, until she spoke, for once without thought of past or future, speaking only for herself, because she wished to.

"I love you, Fred," she whispered.

She had never spoken those words before in her life. Not to her mother. Not to her Aunt April. And now, she had said them to this man, and she couldn't take them back. She felt lighter for having said them, because they were the truth. She wasn't in the habit of telling the truth to anyone, ever.

"What?" he asked.

Clara saw the shock on his face. She fell back on her habitual gesture, shrugging one shoulder, as if to recapture her casual air, but it was gone, and she knew that with him, she would never be casual again.

"I've known for a while. I thought I should tell you."

He kept his gaze focused on her face. "Is that the truth?"

"Have you ever known me to lie to you?"

He drew her close and wrapped his arms around her so tightly that she thought a rib might crack. His lips touched her hair.

"Clara, say it again."

"I love you."

"I'm not going to let you take it back, so make sure you mean it."

Clara laughed, until she looked up and saw his eyes. In the depths of that blue, she lost her smile.

"I love you, Fred. I am never going to take it back."

He kissed her, gently, his lips like feathery moths against her mouth. He held her for a long time, and neither of them spoke. He didn't try to weaken the moment with sex. He didn't move to draw her down onto the couch, and his hands didn't roam over her body. He stood still, breathing in the scent of her hair.

Tension buried at the back of Clara's mind uncoiled and melted away as she stood in his arms. When she took her next breath, the air tasted different. It was the first free breath of air she remembered having drawn in her life. Certainly, the first free breath she'd taken since her mother died, maybe even before that, when Aunt April left. There was no fear in her heart at this moment, and no pain.

"Let me take you somewhere," he said.

Clara didn't hesitate. She didn't think of her planned vacation to Fiji, or of the plane waiting for her on a runway at LAX. She spoke without thought for past or future. She spoke only for herself, and for the joy she felt in that moment.

"All right."

23

NORTHERN CALIFORNIA, 2019

Clara stood under the greenest trees she'd ever seen. She had been born and bred in southern California, and though it was often lush where water was piped in, all the greenery was carefully tended.

The redwoods she stood under now had been there for millennia and stretched so far into the sky that Clara could see no hint of blue. She stood in silence, simply looking at the trees. Some of the trunks were as wide as her car. Clara blinked, her neck aching as she tilted her head back. Fred touched her arm and she turned to look at him, reluctant to take her eyes from the trees.

"I don't know why I never came here before." Her voice was soft, without any pretense of detachment.

She wore no armor for the first time in her life, and she felt naked without it. It was a good feeling.

"It never occurred to you to come here."

Fred's smile warmed her as a fire would. She reached out and ran her fingertips over his lips.

"No. It never occurred to me. I read about these trees once, I think, when I was waiting in a doctor's office."

Fred quirked an eyebrow. "A doctor kept you waiting?"

Clara laughed, feeling younger than she'd ever felt, even when she was a child.

"I wasn't famous at the time."

He took her hand and drew her toward the cabin. She fell into step beside him, still reluctant to come inside from the forest. Fred's house sat five miles outside Crescent City, on the edge of Trinity National Forest. No other houses stood for miles, and he owned the fifteen acres that surrounded his house.

"There's absolutely no one out here, Fred."

Clara stood on the porch of his cabin, drinking in the silence that was broken only by the sound of birds and rustles in the underbrush.

"That's why I bought it. I like to be alone."

Clara turned her gaze to his. "Have you ever been to Palm Springs?"

"Only for the weekend." He waited, his eyes never leaving her face. He knew she had more to say.

She swallowed hard and turned her gaze from him. "I was born there."

He said nothing.

"I grew up there." She waited a moment, and still he didn't speak. "My mother died there when I was sixteen."

Fred stayed silent, but when she didn't speak again, he asked, "Have you been back since?"

Surprised, Clara turned to meet his gaze. His eyes held no pity, only his love for her. She knew he understood that she had never spoken of her mother to another living soul.

"No, I've never been back."

Fred reached out with gentle fingers, and brushed her hair away from her eyes, the same way her Aunt April had touched her long ago.

"Maybe we should go back together."

Clara listened to his voice as he said the word *we*, and she didn't flinch.

"Maybe we should."

Fred said nothing more. He simply reached out and took her hand.

~

Clara watched as a cedar log fell into the center of the fire, releasing a shower of sparks. She sighed and felt Fred's hand touch her hair.

"What are you thinking?" he asked.

She looked at him, surprised at his question. She surprised herself more by answering him. "I was thinking that you are the first person I've trusted in ten years."

His fingers played with a strand of her golden hair. "It's about time, then, wouldn't you say?"

Clara was startled into laughter. "It's past time."

The fire snapped cheerfully, consuming another log.

"I told you before that I don't have any family," she said.

"You told me that."

"It isn't true."

She stopped speaking and the silence between them lengthened. She waited for him to ask her the questions she didn't want to answer, almost holding her breath, wondering what she could bear to tell him. Fred asked nothing, though. He simply kept running his hand through her hair, looking into her eyes as if he expected her to continue speaking.

Clara took a deep breath and spoke. The story of her life came out in a rush, like a river flooding once a dam has broken. She didn't even try to stem the tide but spoke of her mother's marriage and of her aunt's desertion. She spoke of Darren's lust and of her mother's death. She spoke of seeing April in New York only four months before.

Her story ended there, and she sat listening to the silence, waiting for him to speak. She thought he might tell her that she had no heart, that she should reconcile with her aunt and put the old woman out of her misery. She thought he might sympathize with her and tell her how sorry he was that her mother had died, how sorry he was that her mother had never been a true mother to her at all.

Clara waited, but Fred did none of these things. He didn't speak at all. He drew her against him and held her, with one hand on her back and the other stroking her hair. She leaned against him, her muscles tense, still waiting for him to speak, for him to pass judgment on her or to offer her comfort.

As the silence stretched between them, she began to relax, until she leaned against him, boneless, letting him support her weight. The tension flowed out of her body in waves, and she closed her eyes. Just before she fell asleep, she felt his lips on her hair.

"I love you, Clara."

His voice was soft, and if she hadn't been inches away from his mouth, she wouldn't have heard him.

The redwoods rose in a canopy high above their heads. Clara could hear birds singing in the distance, and she raised her face to the sunlight that came through the leaves. Fred stood beside her, his hand on her waist. She smiled at him, and he leaned down and kissed her cheek.

"I can't believe I've never been to this forest before." Clara was surprised to hear how relaxed she sounded.

She couldn't remember the last time she'd felt so at ease with herself or with someone else. It occurred to her that perhaps she never had.

She looked down at the hiking boots Fred had made her buy in town before they'd driven to Trinity National Forest. The boots were brown and fit well with the heavy socks he'd insisted on. Clara laughed at herself. She never let anyone give her orders, and here Fred had given two orders in one day, and he had been obeyed.

The orders had been for her own good. Clara was surprised by that. She was used to looking after her own interests. She had never met another person who put her first, with no thought of personal gain. She paid people to look out for her—her lawyer and Donna and Lila—but Fred did it naturally, without thought. Clara found it intimidating. It called for an equal measure of care from her. She had never actively cared for another person, except perhaps for her mother.

She looked at him and watched the sunlight glint on his dark hair, bringing out the red highlights buried in it. His eyes were shaded from the sun by his glasses as he looked out across the gorge they stood beside. Clara had no way of seeing into his mind, and she was glad. She was forced to take his good will on faith. She was forced to judge him by his actions. So far, he had impressed her.

He turned and caught her staring. She thought he might smile, but he didn't. He stood looking at her, until he reached up and took his glasses off. They faced each other for a long moment, and then he reached up and drew her sunglasses away from her eyes.

"I loved you the moment I saw you," he said.

Clara felt the urge to laugh, to shrug off the seriousness of the moment by refusing to believe him. She also felt the urge to flee down the trail they'd been following. Uneasiness slid into her stomach like a snake. She had never known how to deal with other people's emotions, because she'd never learned to deal with her own.

She decided that for Fred, she would try.

She kept her voice even. "I was a bitch the night you met me, if I recall."

Fred smiled and brushed his fingertips over her cheek, laying his palm against her skin. His hand was warm where he touched her. She didn't take her gaze from his face.

"You've had your moments, I'll say. But I saw through all that."

Clara smiled, reaching up to take his hand in hers. "You did?"

"I did." Fred's smile disappeared. "I knew you were the bravest woman I had ever met and was ever likely to meet."

She almost snorted in derision but controlled herself. "I'm not brave, Fred."

"You are." He said it simply. "I knew there was a lot more to you than what's on the surface."

"And you knew all that from our one encounter in Stan Hendrickson's bathroom."

Fred laughed. "Oh, no. I knew it before I sat next to you by his pool."

She looked into his eyes and felt a question on her tongue that she didn't have the courage to ask. She wondered if he could look into souls the way she could, as her mother had, and her aunt. She was afraid to ask.

"Well, I'm glad you didn't give up on me."

Fred kissed her palm, drawing her back onto the path that led deeper into the forest.

"I love a challenge. And you were worth it."

She didn't know what to say to that, so she said nothing and kissed his cheek.

Together, they walked forward into the trees. Clara no longer felt the need to hide her eyes, so she left her sunglasses in her pocket.

24

MALIBU, 2017

CLARA SMILED TO HERSELF AS HER GUESTS MILLED AROUND, CIRCLING each other warily. She watched them smile at each other and noticed that it often looked as if they were baring their fangs. She shrugged one shoulder. What did she expect, that her first Hollywood party would be different from any other?

Lilies floated in the heated pool and laughter from her house reached her ears. She didn't know many of the people that were there eating her food. Bob had made the guest list, and her assistant, Lila, said everyone was coming.

Clara's new movie, *Queen of Egypt,* was a hit. She knew that was the reason the rich and famous filled her house. They were there to take a look at the flavor of the month. Clara smiled. They didn't realize she was there to stay.

Bob Willoughby moved from his wife's side in the den onto the terrace. Clara leaned back against the railing of her deck and waited for him. She watched as people eyed him with renewed respect. His bid for power at the studio was going well.

Bob took her arm and kissed her cheek. "I'm in, kid."

"In what, Bob?"

He laughed and Clara leaned closer. His gaze never moved from the crowd, and he kept his voice low, as if he expected someone to overhear him.

"I'm head of Barnett Studios."

"You're kidding me."

He grinned at her and winked. "I took over this morning."

She laughed and people turned their heads to look at her. Most of them watched Willoughby, she noticed, though they pretended to smile at her.

"You took over this morning, and you didn't tell me until now?" Clara narrowed her eyes at him, and it was his turn to laugh.

"I wanted to tell you on the terrace of your new house, during the first hour of your first party." Bob leaned down and kissed her cheek. "You were right, kid."

"I'll make you rich, too. Just wait and see."

"I don't think I'll be waiting long, if the numbers on Cleo hold up." He moved off with a little wave. "I'm off to greet my public."

Clara laughed again. She was still laughing when she felt a hand touch her arm. Pete, her old lover, stood at her elbow, looking down at her through his horn-rimmed glasses. He had approached her from behind, so quietly she hadn't heard him.

She smiled at him and took his hand. "Pete, I'm glad you came."

He looked at her and didn't smile. When she opened her mind to find out why, she realized that she hadn't seen him in six months. He hadn't been able to get in touch with her while she was shooting, and after that he hadn't tried. No one had believed him when he said he was a friend. As he stood watching her, he realized for the first time that those people had been right.

Clara saw all this mirrored in his thoughts, and she was tempted to feel guilty, but there were costs to what she was doing. Her relationship with Pete was one casualty. There would be others. When she had remembered him, two weeks ago, she had made sure his name was added to the guest list. She knew now that the gesture wasn't enough.

"Clara. Congratulations."

Clara touched his arm, gently. "Thanks."

"I'm a fool. I shouldn't have come."

He tried to make a casual gesture, waving one hand to encompass her famous guests and her house, but he succeeded only in taking his hand from hers.

Clara didn't smile or look away. "I wouldn't call you a fool."

"This is why you wouldn't marry me, isn't it?" Pete stared at passing staff handing out wine on silver trays.

She knew he meant her newfound fame and all that went with it.

Clara blinked, uncomprehending. She had never realized that he was actually serious all the times he proposed to her. She'd always thought he was making a joke and had laughed it off. Now, as she looked past his surface thoughts for the first time in years, she found in him what she had never found in anyone else.

She felt a stab of pain that took her breath away, because his love for her didn't touch her. It didn't make any difference.

"No, Pete. This isn't why."

"I love you, Clara," he said, simply and with dignity.

She found herself wishing that she loved him back.

Clara squeezed his hand and said nothing. The moment stretched between them, and he simply looked at her as if he were memorizing her face.

"Pete, if you ever need anything, I want you to come to me."

"Anything?"

He quirked an eyebrow at her over his glasses, and she was tempted to laugh, as he intended. She knew, though, that he was leaving and never wanted to see her again.

His smile faded, and he reached out and brushed her cheek with his fingertips. She knew, even as he spoke, that he was lying.

"I will, Clara."

He moved away from her, and she felt a physical pain in her chest. She stood alone in the middle of her party, listening to people she didn't know laugh and drink her wine.

She kept her gaze on Pete as he slipped through the crowd,

speaking to no one, because no one knew him. She stood alone after he disappeared, long after he drove away from her house and was gone.

The film industry was a small town of sorts, but Clara never saw him again.

25

PALM SPRINGS, 2019

THE DESERT STRETCHED TOWARDS THE MOUNTAINS IN THE DISTANCE. Clara remembered from long hikes during her childhood that the desert met the hills and stretched beyond them, too.

She caught herself holding her breath as they drove towards her hometown, and she released it slowly. Fred looked over and offered a smile. He didn't speak, though, and Clara turned back to look out the window of his Jaguar, grateful for the silence. She watched as the buildings of Palm Springs rose before them, low lying structures that were built to stay cool in the searing temperatures of the desert.

Clara found herself fiddling with her gold bracelet as they approached her mother's estate. She stopped, forcing her fingers to lie still. They pulled past the gate and drove up the long drive, past manicured lawns and pinon trees, up to the main house. Fred stopped the Jaguar at the front steps, and Clara didn't move. She felt as if her mother might step out of the house and greet her, waving casually, dressed in her perpetual tennis whites.

Clara sat still and watched as the front door of the house opened. A woman in a business suit greeted Fred as he stepped out of the car. He shook her hand before turning to open Clara's door. Clara looked up at him, frozen in her seat. She didn't think she could force herself to rise. Fred extended a hand to her, and she took it. He helped her stand. Once she was on her feet, she took her hand away and stood on her own.

She turned to look at the house, not hearing the woman as she spoke about the tennis courts, the acres of garden, the marble foyer and the ten Jacuzzi. Clara didn't need her own home described to her.

Fred thanked the woman and asked if they might look around on their own. The realtor agreed and disappeared in the quiet manner of all good servants. Darren had remarried, and his wife wanted him to sell his first wife's estate. Clara noted that the woman had no objection to keeping her mother's millions, however.

Clara walked into the marble foyer through the front door—the door through which her mother's body had been carried out. Her footsteps echoed against the stone, and Clara stopped for a moment, surprised to find the house empty. Of course, Darren had removed the furniture and all her grandmother's antiques.

She walked on and heard Fred behind her. He didn't move to take her arm or to speak to her, and again she was grateful. She stepped into the conservatory, looking through the glass walls into the garden. She could see the desert shimmering beyond the pinon trees at the edge of the lawn.

"I'd like to go outside," she said.

"All right."

Fred opened the door to the terrace, and Clara led the way as they walked through the lush garden. The plants were just as her mother had left them. Darren had little use for gardens and hadn't bothered to change anything.

Clara kept walking, and Fred followed her until they reached the edge of the lawn and stood in the brown desert rock with bits of shifting sand blowing past them.

"It's beautiful here." Fred's voice was quiet.

Clara turned to look at him. "It is beautiful, isn't it?"

He reached out and touched her hair, letting his hand slide along her cheek. She turned her head and pressed her lips into his palm.

"Do you want to see more of the house, Clara?"

She felt the play of emotions as they crossed her face. Two weeks ago, she would have made sure her expression was a bland mask. At best, she would have given him a sardonic smile. Now, she allowed her pain to rise into her eyes as she looked at him.

"No. I remember what the house looks like. I just wanted to see the desert again."

He took her in his arms and held her. They watched as the sand blew in patterns across the rock face in front of them, the slanting sun casting their shadows toward the mountains far to the east.

The old landline was ringing when they walked into Clara's house, and she picked up the receiver. Margherita had long since gone home, and the lights of the yachts were bright on Malibu bay.

"Hello?"

"Clara, you're home. Where have you been?"

She frowned for a moment, trying to place the voice.

"Clara, it's me, Chuck. Where were you?"

She smiled. Only her favorite director would call her house, ignoring her cell.

"It doesn't matter. What's up?"

"I've got a job for you."

She chuckled. "Chuck, you're not playing the game. Your people are supposed to call Donna and tell her that. Then she calls me, then I say yes, and then she relays that back through your people, to you. That's how it's done."

"So you'll do it?"

"I'd work for you if you were doing a story about laundry detergent. Yes, I'll do it."

"Great!"

Clara heard the joy in his voice, and that it was genuine.

"I can't pay you as much as last time."

"Oh, I know that. Last time the studio was kissing my ass. This time, they'll be back to business."

Fred smiled at her from the lighted foyer, where he leaned against the mahogany-paneled wall, watching her.

"It's a great script, Clara. It's a story of a mother and daughter who reconcile after years of animosity."

"And I'm playing the mother?"

Chuck snorted on the other end of the phone. "Seriously, Clara, you're going to love it."

"I know I will. Messenger it over in the morning and let Donna know when you'll need me to sign the contract."

"You don't want to see the script tonight?"

Clara almost laughed at the eagerness in Chuck's voice, but her respect for him kept her silent. She leaned back into Fred's arms as his lips trailed down her throat.

"Not tonight, Chuck. Tomorrow will be soon enough."

Early the next morning, Fred found Clara standing on the terrace, looking out over the bay. She had given Margherita and the rest of the staff the day off, and now she was brooding.

He pressed one hand against her lower back, and she tilted her head for his kiss. He could see she was still preoccupied and rubbed her shoulder.

"I've read the script," she said.

"Already?" Fred raised an eyebrow. "When did Chuck send it?"

"It got here about dawn. He probably thought the staff would be here." She leaned against the railing and looked out over the blue waters of the bay.

There had been rain yesterday, and the pollution that usually hung over the water had washed out to sea.

"What did you think of the script?"

"It's brilliant."

Clara turned to him, her face unreadable except for the pain in her eyes. "The story is about a mother who's never around, and her adult daughter who chooses to forgive her."

"That hits close to home."

155

"I never said I forgave my mother."

"No. You never said so."

Clara looked at him and expected to feel anger rise up to choke her. She didn't feel angry, though, and she realized he was right. She had forgiven her mother long ago. Her mother had been so selfish that she truly hadn't seen anyone or anything else beyond what she wanted. But her aunt had been her mainstay and her haven, the one person she was sure would never leave her.

It was April's abandonment she couldn't forgive.

Clara leaned against him, resting her head on his chest as he stroked her hair. Fred spoke as if he'd heard exactly what she was thinking. He did that from time to time, and by now it seemed natural.

"Maybe your aunt will see the movie once it's done."

"My aunt doesn't go to the movies."

"She may go to this one."

"Fred, stay out of it."

He ran his hands over her body. "Come back to bed."

"Read the script first."

"It's that good?"

"Yes."

He took her hand, drawing her into the house. "I'll read it now."

26

MALIBU, 2020

CLARA PICKED UP HER CELL ON THE FIRST RING. MARGHERITA AND Paolo had left for the evening, and Fred hadn't come home yet. She'd spent the day lying beside the pool, her first quiet day since her public relations tour to advertise her newest film, *Slow Rise*.

"Clara?"

Donna sounded breathless on the other end of the line, and Clara smiled. Her manager never hurried unless something important was brewing.

"Hi, Donna. How was your trip to Biarritz?"

"Great, fine, yeah, great. Listen, I've got news."

"You're pregnant."

Donna choked on a sip of her bourbon. "Hell, no."

Clara listened to her splutter and covered the receiver so Donna wouldn't hear her laughing.

"No, Clara, it's much bigger than that."

"What?"

"You've been nominated—"

"For a People's Choice Award. I know. My public is ever faithful."

"No, listen to this." Donna took a deep breath.

Clara even heard her put her drink down.

"You have been nominated for a SAG award."

Clara listened for a long moment to the silence on the line. She didn't think she'd heard right.

"Donna, come on, that's bullshit."

"No, really, Clara. I wouldn't bullshit you about anything, but especially not something like this. The Screen Actors Guild nominated you. They called and told me today. It's going to be announced in the morning."

Clara's eyes narrowed. "Who called and told you?"

Donna picked up her drink again and rattled the ice in the glass. "I really can't say."

"So, they're announcing it tomorrow, and you know about it today."

"Yes."

"Holy shit."

"Congratulations, Clara."

Clara blinked at the sincere admiration in her manager's voice.

"You really deserve it."

"Thanks, Donna."

Fred came in the front door, carrying a dozen roses, all yellow with pink tips.

"I've got to go," Clara said. "Thanks for telling me. I'll see you tomorrow."

"Call me about what you want to wear. We'll go see some designers next week."

"OK, Donna. Thanks."

Clara hung up, watching Fred put the roses down with a flourish.

"You will not believe this," she said.

"Try me." He grinned, his eyes gleaming as he pressed a kiss on her throat.

"The Guild nominated me for my performance in *Slow Rise*."

Fred kept grinning. "That's what I heard."

"How is it that you and Donna know, and I have no clue?"

"That's the business, kid."

She punched him in the arm, but he just held her tighter.

❧

Chuck gave Clara a kiss on the cheek. They stood backstage at the Screen Actors Guild Awards. Clara had already accepted her award for Best Female Actor in a Feature Film. She was shocked that she'd won. Most people in Hollywood watched her films and rolled their eyes. Of course, the last film Chuck had made was different from all the others.

"Clara, congratulations again. You deserve it."

"Thanks, Chuck." Clara smiled at him, resisting the urge to brush his bangs back from his eyes.

"I've got another project I want to talk to you about."

"Chuck, I'm going to be taking a few months off."

"Oh, that's great! I need about six months to get the script finished."

"You're writing it yourself?" Clara raised an eyebrow.

"I've written it already. I'm re-writing it now to see if I can get something that the studio and I can both live with."

Clara laughed at that. "If anybody can, you will. You'll probably end up getting an Oscar for it."

He blushed, and Clara smiled at him.

"Just say you'll look at it when it's ready."

"You know I will."

A willowy woman walked up to him, offering him her hand. She was to direct him back to his seat. He wasn't a member of the Guild, but Clara had gotten him into the award banquet anyway.

"I'll see you at Bob's party after?" Chuck asked as he moved away.

"You will."

Fred came up behind Clara, brandishing her trophy.

"Fred, I thought you were going to stay in the audience and smile supportively in case they get you on camera while I'm presenting."

He chuckled, running his free hand down her back. "I'd rather be back here with you."

Clara turned to him, her gaze fastened on his lips. "Do you think we could sneak off somewhere and neck before I have to go on?"

He laughed. "I don't think we have time."

He ran his hand over the silk of her dress, brushing his fingers over her bare back. Clara shivered.

"Clara, I need to tell you something."

She smiled at his serious tone. She couldn't remember the last time she'd felt so light-hearted.

"What?" she asked.

"Your aunt is out there."

"What?"

"Your Aunt April is in the audience."

Clara took a deep breath and released it slowly.

Fred kept his gaze on her face. "She wanted a ticket, and I got her one."

"She came alone?"

"Yes."

Clara leaned against him. "You shouldn't have interfered, Fred."

"Yes, I should have."

She met his gaze and saw nothing but love for her in his eyes.

"It was high-handed."

"That's right."

"No one gets in my family's business."

"I just did."

Clara sighed deeply, suddenly feeling tired.

"She loved the movie, sweetheart. She wants to see you again. I want you to talk to her afterwards."

Clara shifted her gaze to the woman striding toward her. "I'll think about it."

"That's all I ask."

She felt his lips brush her hair. Then she was moving towards the stage. She stepped onto it, greeted by applause as she walked under the hot lights. She smiled her studio smile for the cameras she couldn't see. She stood at the podium, speaking easily to the crowd of actors in front of her, some of whom she actually respected.

As she spoke, she looked out over the crowd, and past the bank of lights, she saw April sitting by herself, with the Shakespearean actor James Simpson on one side of her and Pat Mulligan on the other. Both men were not watching the stage, but had their gazes set on her aunt. Clara looked down at the envelope in her hand so she wouldn't lose her train of thought and get distracted by April's conquests.

When she looked up again, she met her aunt's gaze over the distance that stretched between them. April's eyes were bright, and Clara knew that they were full of unshed tears. She felt the same tears in her own eyes and wondered what the people watching on television would make of them. Surely, they would not believe that she was moved by the Best Female Actor in a Miniseries.

Clara read the name of the woman who had won the award and stepped back as she came to collect it. As the woman made her speech, Clara's gaze never left her aunt's face. As she watched, April dabbed at her eyes, and Pat Mulligan leaned over and offered her a handkerchief from his pocket. Her aunt accepted it graciously.

April and Clara smiled at each other, and Clara felt her heart lighten. She moved off stage, with the winner of the award in tow. When she reached Fred's side, she kissed his cheek.

"Does this mean you'll see her?" he asked.

"Yes."

Fred took her in his arms and kissed her, oblivious to the people standing around them. Clara didn't pull away.

27

MALIBU, 2020

Clara sank into the Jacuzzi and sighed. The warm water bubbled around her, soothing her tired muscles. She felt good, but it had been a long night. Facing her aunt in the lobby after the ceremony had been harder than she'd expected.

She could still feel her aunt's cool lips on her cheek. Fred had stood by, close enough to be supportive, but far enough away to give them a moment of privacy.

Aunt April had looked serene in her blue silk gown, her hair swept up in the inevitable French twist. Pat Mulligan had looked at her aunt with more than a little interest, but April hadn't noticed.

April touched Clara's hand. "I'm proud of you, Clara."

"Thank you." She took a deep breath, knowing she couldn't allow herself to cry in front of all these actors, some of whom wished her ill.

"Your mother would have been proud of you."

Clara swallowed hard, dropping her gaze to the crimson carpet. Fred stepped forward, putting his hand on the small of her back. She felt his strength flow into her, and she straightened, her eyes dry. There were no words to bridge the span of ten years, to bridge that

162

span of loss and pain. It was with that touch that Clara took the first step.

Clara, who never touched a woman voluntarily, who guarded herself like a citadel, reached out and kissed her aunt's cheek. Aunt April held herself still. Though her eyes were luminous, April smiled.

She pressed her niece's hand. "My driver's waiting for me. I have a flight to catch."

"Of course."

April touched her cheek. "I'm going to Palm Springs. I'd like you to join me there for a day, if you can spare the time."

Clara felt Fred's hand press heavily into her back, and she smiled. She didn't need his prompting.

"Of course, I'll come," she heard herself say.

People were waiting to congratulate her, so April squeezed her hand and disappeared into the crowd.

Clara spent the rest of the evening shaking hands, kissing cheeks, and thanking everyone for their good wishes and their votes. She couldn't remember later who she'd seen that night after her aunt left, except for Pat Mulligan. He'd kissed her hand and whispered congratulations in her ear in the soft burr that always made her shiver. She saw Fred frown as Pat wandered away, and she laughed.

"He's married, Fred."

He looked down at her with a sardonic smile. "Since when has that ever stopped you?"

She turned and kissed him, heedless of the people watching them. "I stopped doing that sort of thing when I started seeing you."

He drew her against him, his arm around her waist. He kept his arm around her until Donna got them to the car that waited for them outside. Donna smiled to see Clara so obviously in love but knew better than to comment on it.

"I'll call you tomorrow, Clara."

"Not before noon."

Donna laughed with a sidelong glance at Fred. "Of course not."

Clara laughed, too, as the limousine pulled away from the curb.

Her thoughts came back to the present as she leaned against the edge of the tub, watching Fred step naked out of her bedroom and onto the cedar wood deck. She watched the play of his muscles as he slid into the water beside her. He handed her a glass of chardonnay, kissing her. She took the wine but pulled back from the kiss. If he was surprised, he didn't show it, but sat back and watched her.

Clara looked up into the night sky. A few feeble stars could be seen beyond the bright lights from the city. A warm breeze stirred her hair, and she sighed. Fred sat as if waiting for her to speak. She stared back at him in the candlelight, taking a sip of her wine.

"Fred, I need a straight answer from you."

"That's good. I only give straight answers."

"How did you know I wanted to see my aunt again?"

He didn't answer, but drank his wine, then set it on the rim of the Jacuzzi.

"I've made a point of avoiding her almost all my life, but somehow you knew I wanted to see her, in spite of that."

Fred shrugged one shoulder, a gesture she knew he'd picked up from her.

"I took a gamble."

"I don't think so. You never gamble. Everything you do, you always know what the outcome will be before you do it."

"Clara—"

She held up a hand, and he fell silent. "Let me finish. You knew that your other project would make more money for the studio than my costume drama. My drama made a lot of money, thanks to Chuck, but your space thriller made more."

"That's just knowing the market, Clara."

She looked at him, her gaze not leaving his face. He looked back at her, and the silence stretched between them. She spoke again, sensing that he was ready to tell her the truth.

"It was more than market research, wasn't it, Fred?" Her voice was deceptively calm.

She could feel the rapid beat of her pulse, and she took a deep breath in an effort to steady it.

He didn't look away from her. "Yes, it was more than research."

Clara felt a little light-headed, and she knew it was more than exhaustion. For the first time in her life, she was afraid. She couldn't remember ever having been afraid before, except perhaps while she was watching her mother die.

"You can see into people's heads, can't you?" she asked.

Fred was silent for a moment, running his fingertips over the rim of his wine glass.

"What do you mean, exactly?"

"When you look at a person, you can see behind their eyes. You can see what their thoughts are, what motivates them, what they want and how they plan to get it. You can see into their souls."

"I usually don't look that deep."

His answer stood alone in the silence that followed. Clara could hear the chiming of the grandfather clock from its perch in her living room. She could hear, distantly, the sound of traffic on the highway. She couldn't hear his thoughts, just as she never could.

"You looked into my soul, didn't you?"

He didn't flinch or look away from her. "Yes."

Clara sat still. She had suspected he had the gift, and now she knew. She was numb, as if she'd run a mile through the snow without boots. She knew that pain would follow when the numbness wore off.

Fred was touching her, and his hands felt the same as they always had. He tilted her chin until she was looking into his eyes. He held her gaze and wouldn't let her look away.

"Clara, I love you. I saw into your mind the first night I met you, and I've loved you ever since."

"You can see all of me. And you always have." Clara's voice was accusing, but she didn't pull away. She sounded like an angry child to her own ears. She thought for a moment that she might weep.

He drew her closer to him on the bench and cradled her head against his chest. "That isn't such a bad thing, Clara. You're just learning to see good things about yourself. I saw them from the beginning."

"You know that I can read people, too?"

"Yes, but I don't know why you've never been able to read me. If you had, we would have been together a long time ago, I think."

Clara laughed in spite of herself. "No, I would have run you out of town."

He laughed with her. "The hell you would have. There's room enough in this town for two seers."

Clara was quiet for a while, her mind numb, her heart full, listening to the sound of the ocean below her house as it rose and fell, its eternal motion soothing her, lulling her, just as his hands did as they touched her. She wasn't able to see into his mind or his soul, so she would have to trust herself and trust him. She would have to rely on her instincts.

"How do you know we're the only ones?" she asked, her fear and anger slipping away in the warmth of his smile.

"I don't."

He saw the look of horror on her face, and smiled.

28

PALM SPRINGS, 2020

CLARA STOOD ON THE FRONT TERRACE OF HER MOTHER'S HOUSE. She had come alone, as April had requested. Fred was going to follow later that morning, giving her a little time with her aunt in her childhood home.

Clara looked out over the front lawn, which was as manicured as it had ever been. The green shown like deep velvet, and where the sprinklers had been running, Clara could see the water collecting like dew. April's rented Lincoln was parked in the circular driveway. Clara waited for the real estate woman to appear, but no one came.

The front door of the house opened, and April stepped out. The house key was on the same plastic ring the real estate woman had held the last time Clara had been there.

April stood in the doorway, silent. Clara heard the air conditioner humming deep within the house.

"I'm early." Clara's voice was hoarse.

She cleared her throat, finding it difficult to speak to April after so many years apart. They had left so much unsaid for so long that simple conversation was an effort.

Clara noticed a glint of silver in her aunt's hair as April turned her head to look out over the front lawn, and she remembered her mother. Jessica would have colored her hair rather than let silver show.

April met Clara's gaze. "I'm glad you're here."

She stepped into the house, and Clara followed her, though she found herself reluctant to walk into that house again. She wondered who had bought it, and how she was going to stand being there with her aunt again, even for an hour.

Clara walked inside, and April closed the heavy mahogany door behind her.

"Will you come into the conservatory?" April asked. "I know it was your favorite room."

"All right."

The morning sunlight slanted in through the heavy plate glass windows. The room was hot as it always was, in spite of the air conditioner running at full speed. Clara smiled as she looked through the windows. She could see the desert shimmering at the edge of the garden. Many things changed, but the desert was always there. The sight of it, and the feel of that heat, gave her comfort.

Clara spoke, her words coming more easily than they had before. "Mother's ashes were scattered over that desert."

"I know."

She turned to look at her aunt and saw the pain in her face. "Did you hate my mother, April?"

April started to cry, silently, but her expression didn't change. The tears just ran in streams down her cheeks. She blinked to see past them but took no other notice of them.

"I loved her very much."

"I wonder if she loved you." Clara was surprised at her own cruelty.

She didn't take the words back once they were spoken but let them linger between them. The twelve-year-old who still lived inside her wanted to hear her aunt's answer.

"We'll never know that, Clara."

"No, I guess we won't."

Clara stepped over to the window and pressed her hand against the glass. It was hot to the touch. The mountains in the distance looked like a mirage as the morning heat rose in front of them in waves.

Clara spoke again, her voice low. "I wonder if she loved me."

April reached out for her sister's daughter. Clara found herself in her aunt's embrace, and she stood stiffly for a long moment, unable to breathe. Then the scent of her aunt's perfume slipped past her defenses, and she sighed, leaning against her. She hadn't touched April that way since her twelfth birthday, the day she'd gone away.

Her aunt's arms were the haven they'd been in her childhood. Her aunt was thin and her arms bony, but Clara had never felt as safe anywhere else. Not with any man other than Fred, and certainly not with any woman. The apple green silk of April's suit was soft against Clara's cheek.

April's tears had stopped. "Jessica made a lot of bad choices, but she always loved you."

Clara drew back to look into her aunt's face. She opened herself to peer into her aunt's mind, to see if she was telling the truth. As always, her aunt's mind was a closed door.

April laid her hand against Clara's cheek, wiping the tears away. Clara wasn't sure if April was telling the truth, but she did know that her aunt wanted her to believe that Jessica had loved her, in spite of all appearances to the contrary.

Perhaps Jessica had loved her daughter the way a spoiled child loves a favorite doll, a doll that it only now and then remembers to bring out of its toy chest.

For the first time in Clara's life, the memory of her mother didn't bring her pain. She smiled at her aunt, and April pulled away, reaching into her Hermes bag. Clara started to reach for her own purse, but April stopped her, wiping Clara's tears away with her own handkerchief. Clara stood still and let her do it.

April wiped away all traces of her own tears. "I have news, Clara."

"What is it?"

April's smile was bright and devoid of pain. "I've bought the house."

"What house?"

"This one. Your mother's house. My mother's house."

Clara stepped back, her knees weak. She would have sat on the parquet floor but stayed upright from long habit of supporting herself.

"You bought this house?"

April laughed a little, tossing her head so that her earrings danced. "Do you think I would let some stranger buy it? Your mother was born in this house. Did you know that, Clara?"

"No, I didn't."

"She was born here because Mother was too stubborn to go into town. She insisted on having her at home. She said the doctors hadn't done a thing to help her when I was born, and she'd be damned if she'd leave the comfort of her bed to convenience them a second time." April laughed. "So Daddy brought a bevy of doctors out here. Of course, by the time he got back with them, your mom was already born and wrapped in a blanket." April laughed harder. "Daddy was fit to be tied. Mother just said, 'Do you expect me to hold up nature for you, Seymour?' "

Clara laughed at that. She had never before heard any stories about her grandparents. She took in the knowledge and filed it away so she might draw it out again later, when she was alone.

April opened the terrace door, and they stepped outside. "Would you like to walk to the desert?" she asked.

Clara nodded, and they fell into step beside each other, the cool grass under their feet warring with the heat of the morning.

"I'm going to live here for part of the year from now on." April didn't miss a step. "I want you to have a key so you can come here whenever you want. Hollywood may be tough to take, from time to time. When it is, you can come home."

Clara stopped walking. She looked into her aunt's eyes and found that her voice had deserted her.

April lost her smile. "Promise me you'll come."

"I will. I promise."

They walked the rest of the way to the desert in silence. That was where Fred found them half an hour later. Two slender women standing together on the edge of the desert, sunlight glinting on their blonde hair.

They watched as the sun rose above the mountains in the distance. It blinded them with its radiance.

Dear reader,

We hope you enjoyed reading *The Slow Rise of Clara Daniels*. Please take a moment to leave a review in Amazon, even if it's a short one. Your opinion is important to us.

Discover more books by Christy English at https://www. nextchapter.pub/authors/christy-english

Want to know when one of our books is free or discounted for Kindle? Join the newsletter at http://eepurl.com/bqqB3H

Best regards,

Christy English and the Next Chapter Team

ABOUT THE AUTHOR

A graduate of Duke University, Christy English is the author of the historical fiction novels *The Queen's Pawn* (2010) and *To Be Queen: A Novel of The Early Life of Eleanor of Aquitaine* (2011), from New American Library, a division of Penguin Random House. She has also written two historical romance series for Sourcebooks Casablanca—*Shakespeare in Love* (2012-2013) and *Broadswords and Ballrooms* (2015-2016). When she's not writing, she loves to walk the mountain trails near her home in western North Carolina.

You might also like:
What Comes Of Eating Doughnuts With A Boy Who Plays Guitar by Nicole Campbell

To read the first chapter for free go to:

https://www.nextchapter.pub/books/what-comes-of-eating-doughnuts

9 781034 269144